"You want me as much as I want you."

Rex continued determinedly. "The way you kissed me proves that. So why this act of playing hard to get?"

"Hard to get? I've only known you a week!" Harriet's voice trembled. "I don't go to bed with men I've just met. And I'm not going to bed with you just because you happen to be America's number five sex symbol. Anyway, in my book it's called making love, and there has to be real emotion involved."

"So you want it all dressed up as romance," Rex said derisively. "But I'm not going to make it easy for you by saying I'm in love with you. You're going to go to bed with me, Harry—and on my terms, not on yours."

SALLY WENTWORTH began her publishing career at a Fleet Street newspaper in London, where she thrived in the hectic atmosphere. After her marriage, she and her husband moved to rural Hertfordshire, where Sally had been raised. Although she worked for the publisher of a group of magazines, the day soon came when her own writing claimed her energy and time. Her romance novels are often set in fascinating foreign locales.

Books by Sally Wentworth

Don't miss any of our special offers. Write to us at the following address for information on our newest releases.

Harlequin Reader Service
901 Fuhrmann Blvd., P.O. Box 1397, Buffalo, NY 14240
Canadian address: P.O. Box 603,
Fort Erie, Ont. L2A 5X3

SALLY WENTWORTH

dishonourable intentions

Harlequin Books

TORONTO • NEW YORK • LONDON
AMSTERDAM • PARIS • SYDNEY • HAMBURG
STOCKHOLM • ATHENS • TOKYO • MILAN

Harlequin Presents first edition July 1988
ISBN 0-373-11094-4

Original hardcover edition published in 1987
by Mills & Boon Limited

CHAPTER ONE

'OK, GIRLS. Now you've all read the script and you know the basic plot: a young American girl who is living in London gets murdered and her fiancé comes over to try to find out who did it. And he starts by suspecting her three flat-mates. Played by you three.'

The director paused to look at the faces of the young actresses listening to him intently and nodded approvingly; the casting department had chosen well. These girls were all keen and had enough experience to take direction, but not so much that they would try to push their own ideas for the parts on him.

'We intend to shoot most of the studio scenes first,' he went on, 'and do the location shots later. Now today, after you've been to wardrobe, I want you to familiarise yourselves with the sets we've erected of the London flat where most of the action takes place. You've been given a shooting schedule, and you'll see that we're going to spend the first few days doing the scenes leading up to the murder. So I want you all to know your lines ready for tomorrow morning. OK. Now, do any of you have any questions?' he asked, looking round.

Harriet Sutton shook her head decisively when the director's eyes met hers; she had already studied the script so thoroughly that she was word-perfect in nearly every scene in the film in which the character she played, a girl called Nicky Wells, was to appear.

'I have a question,' one of the other girls offered. Her name, Harriet recalled, was Emma Page and she was short and blonde. 'When does Rex Kynaston get here? I'm dying to meet him!'

The director and the other girls laughed at her enthusiasm. 'Not for another week,' the director answered. 'He's tied up with his television series until then. But when he does arrive we'll give him a welcome party so that you can all meet him. Has anyone any other questions?'

No one had, so the three of them, Harriet, Emma, and the third girl, Julie Baxter, all left the director's office and made their way through the big film studio to wardrobe.

'Isn't this just great?' Emma said excitedly, clutching her script to her chest.

Harriet nodded. 'It certainly is. It's one of the best breaks I've ever had. I've mostly done television and theatre work before, except for one film that was a complete flop. How about you two?'

'I had a small part in a film about eighteen months ago, but that was a miserable failure, too,' Julie answered. 'I just hope this one is more successful.'

'With a big star like Rex Kynaston in it, it's bound to be,' Emma answered exultantly. 'He's sure to draw the crowds to the box office. Have you seen him on television? Isn't he gorgeous? But I'm petrified of acting with him, in case I'm so overwhelmed that I just dry up.'

The other two girls laughed at her. They had only met that day, the first day of filming of *Madam, Will You Talk?* when the cast and crew had gathered to meet each other. All except Rex Kynaston, of course, the big name that the producers were relying on to turn their venture into a success.

At the wardrobe department they tried on the clothes that had been chosen for them for the first weeks of filming. They were the kind of clothes that any girl working in London would wear. Smart and fashionable, but nothing too glamorous or expensive. As the woman who was fitting them pointed out when Julie looked at them distastefully, they were to play ordinary working girls, not taking part in some glamorous American soap opera.

After they had tried on the clothes to the wardrobe mistress's satisfaction, the girls automatically stayed together and went over to the restaurant for lunch.

'I don't dare eat too much,' Emma said with a sigh as she ordered a salad. 'I put on weight so quickly.' She looked at Harriet wistfully. 'You're so thin. How do you manage it?'

Harriet looked up from the double-decker hamburger that she was about to bite into and shrugged. 'I don't know. I can eat anything and never put on weight. I think it's something to do with your metabolism; you either stay thin all your life or you put on weight. It's just the luck of the draw. If this had been the eighteenth or nineteenth century when it was fashionable to be plump, I'd have been envious of you.'

'That's no comfort,' Emma said with a gloomy face, chewing unhappily on a lettuce leaf. 'How are you two going to get to work?' she asked after a moment. 'My home is in Birmingham, so it's too far for me to travel every day. At the moment, I'm staying in a hotel. How about you, Harriet?'

'Why don't you call me Harry? Everyone does,' Harriet said with one of her warm smiles. 'I live in London, so it isn't too far to drive here. And I'm going in the opposite direction to all the rush-hour traffic, which is a help.'

'I drive myself as well,' Julie told them. 'My husband has to take the train instead, but we're hoping to be able to afford a car each once I start getting paid for this film.'

'You're married?' Emma exclaimed. 'How does your husband feel about you working with a macho sex symbol like Rex Kynaston? Is he jealous?'

Julie laughed. 'Not really, but he's getting teased a lot. But it's not as if I have any love scenes with him. Harry's the one he has to try and seduce.'

They both looked rather enviously at Harriet and she said quickly, 'Don't look at me like that. It's only a part. And Rex Kynaston is such a sex symbol that he's bound to hog all the best camera shots. All the public will see of me will probably be the back of my head!'

'Do you really think he's going to be like that? Play at being the big star and everything?' Emma wondered.

'Well, of course he is,' Harry returned. 'Why, just look at the treatment he's getting here! The film company have booked him into a flat in one of the most luxurious blocks in London. *And* they've laid on a limousine to drive him around everywhere. *And* they've agreed to fly him back to America any weekend he wants to go. *And* he's getting a huge salary. *And* he's getting a big slice of the box office receipts...'

Julie held up a hand. 'OK, OK. We get the picture. How do you know all this?'

'One of the men I live with happens to be a reporter on a national daily; he...'

'*One* of the men you live with?' Emma interrupted, bug-eyed.

'What? Oh, no, it's nothing like that. Four of us share a house in London. Two guys and two girls. But I'm the only girl at the moment. It's just a convenient arrangement. And, as I said, one of them heard about the deal Rex Kynaston was getting through someone who works on his paper and has contacts with the film world. They couldn't print it, though, because they couldn't get to see any written evidence to verify the rumour.'

'Well, I suppose he's worth that much if it means that the film will be a hit,' Julie remarked.

'Nobody's worth that much,' Harry disagreed forcefully. 'If these so-called big stars didn't demand such huge salaries, the film companies could afford to make twice as many films, and to experiment with new ideas. All they do now is play safe and pick scripts which they know will appeal to the majority of cinema-goers. So you just get the same kind of thing over and over again.'

'Wow! I wish I hadn't said anything,' Julie said in a rather taken-aback tone.

'Oh, dear! I'm sorry.' Harry's hazel eyes lit with laughter. 'I'm afraid that's one of my pet hobby-horses.'

Emma grinned. 'Do you have many of them?'

Harriet's mouth widened into a delighted laugh. 'Quite a few, I'm afraid.'

The eyes of the two other girls were drawn to her face for a long moment. They were both good-looking girls: Emma short and blonde, Julie of average height and with stunning red hair, but Harriet, when her face grew animated, was more than pretty. Her clear hazel eyes were set in an oval face with perfect bone structure, a wide forehead, high cheekbones, straight nose and softly rounded chin. Her eyebrows were finely arched, and she had long dark lashes that complemented her dark hair, which was cut in a thick, slightly long page-boy style that brushed her shoulders. In repose her face was serene, but when it grew animated it revealed vitality and intelligence, an innate love of life that shone in her face, attracting everyone who saw her.

After they'd eaten, the girls went back to the big studio and walked around the sets that had been erected to show the parts of a London flat: the corridor outside, the front door and hall, a small kitchen, the sitting-room and a bedroom. Harry found it quite easy to familiarise herself with the layouts, because she was used to doing film and television work, but Emma, who had done mostly stage work, found it more difficult.

'I know I'm just going to be useless at this kind of acting,' she said worriedly.

'No, you won't,' Harriet encouraged her. 'Basically, you have to remember just to speak normally and not to pitch your voice for an audience. And you'll soon get so used to the cameras that you'll forget they're there.'

When they'd studied the layout of the set they were free to go, so the three girls walked to the car park, again automatically sticking together on their first day. They felt very much the new girls, as it seemed that nearly all the crew and most of the production staff had worked together two or three times before. Only the actors were coming together for the first time.

They went to the car park, Julie and Harry to take their cars to drive home, and Emma to walk to her hotel, which was only a short distance away. However, after

Julie had gone, Emma hovered beside Harry, reluctant to be left on her own.

'Good heavens! Is this your car?' she exclaimed as Harriet stopped by a low-slung sports car and took some keys from her bag.

'Yes, it's an early Lotus.' There was pride in Harry's voice. She loved cars and always had, sharing the love with her father and two elder brothers, who were all mad keen and spent most of their time either working on cars or racing them, liking nothing better than to restore a rusting old wreck back into working order. Her Lotus was over twenty years old, and she was very proud of the fact that she had completely restored it herself. She smiled at Emma. 'See you tomorrow, then.'

The other girl nodded brightly, but then looked anxious again. 'I hope I get here on time. Seven o'clock is so very early when you've been used to theatre work. I'd hate to be late on my first day.'

'Tell the hotel receptionist to give you an early-morning call. They've probably had loads of actors staying there who've been working at the studios, so they'll be used to waking people and giving them an early breakfast.'

'That's a point,' Emma agreed, cheering up. ''Bye, Harry.'

The film studios were situated in Hertfordshire, a county just north of London, in a town where films had been made right back to the nineteen-thirties. Although its fortunes had fluctuated quite a lot, and the biggest studios had closed down and been converted into ware-housing, the film industry still had a hold there, even though most of the remaining studios were now used for television productions. There was a good road link from

the town into central London, and Harry was able to
put her foot down and drive right up to the speed limit
until the roads became more crowded as she neared the
centre of town. She lived in a terraced house in a quiet,
tree-lined street at the Notting Hill Gate end of Kensington, an area that hadn't become so fashionable that
it was expensive and hadn't gone downhill so that it was
disreputable. Many of the surrounding streets hovered
on the brink of becoming either one, but so far the street
in which Harriet lived had managed to stay nicely in the
middle. She drove round to the back of the terrace and
locked her car away in a garage; the area wasn't safe
enough for her to leave it out on the street at night, and
the car was far too precious to her to take any risks of
having it vandalised.

The house was empty as she'd expected, so after she'd
fed the cats she changed and did some housework before
starting to cook dinner. Usually, Harry and her fellow
tenants took it in turns to prepare the evening meal, but
as they were one girl short and she was home early
anyway, Harriet went ahead with it herself. She made a
casserole, the savoury smell of which drifted to the front
door an hour or so later when Bob Stonor, the reporter
she had told Emma and Julie about, came home.

"Lo, Harry. Mm, that smells good.' He dropped a
briefcase on to the floor and came into the kitchen to
pour himself a drink. 'God, I needed that.'

Any other woman would probably have been immediately sympathetic and asked him if he'd had a hard
day, but Harriet didn't see why she should drop into a
traditionally feminine role just because she happened to
share a house with two people who happened to be men,
so she merely said, 'Pour me one, too, will you?' Then

added pointedly, 'And we need a new light bulb in the fitting on the landing.'

Bob grinned, quite used to the way Harry treated him after living with her for nearly two years. He liked her very much, and at first had been half inclined to fall in love with her, but her practical, no-nonsense attitude towards him had made them close friends instead. He had a great respect for her, too, knowing that she was perfectly capable of changing the bulb herself and of doing almost any job around the house better than he could, using her brain where he would use brute strength. But she was tactful about it so that he didn't feel inferior or unmanned, hiding her competence and independence beneath an outward face of softness and femininity. So neither Bob nor Eric, the third tenant of the house, was *in* love with her, but they both loved Harry as a friend and were fiercely protective of her.

It wasn't until Eric had come home, and the three of them were sitting down to dinner, that they talked about the good or bad things that life had dealt them that day. Eric was an engineer and was a large, quiet man of twenty-eight. He didn't have a lot to say himself, but listened with humour as Bob recounted the story he'd been sent to follow up, which had turned out to be a wild-goose chase.

'It was just a completely false lead,' Bob said disgustedly. 'Somebody with a grudge obviously phoned it in just to waste the paper's time.' He turned to Harry. 'I hope your day went better.'

'Much better,' she smiled. 'The girls I'm to work with seem very nice, and I think making the film is going to be great fun.'

'And what did you think of Rex Kynaston in the flesh?' Bob asked, but not without a slight touch of sarcastic envy in his tone. 'Is he as macho as he appears on television?'

Harriet shook her head. 'He wasn't there. He doesn't arrive in England until next week. The producers are going to give a party for him and all the cast have been invited, so I'll let you know then.' She picked up her glass to take a drink, smiling inwardly; it was surprising how uptight and jealous men seemed to get when women talked about a sex symbol like Rex Kynaston, almost as if they felt their masculinity was threatened. Which was crazy really; tough, larger-than-life men like that were OK as screen heroes, but what woman in her right mind would seriously want to get mixed up with one? No woman who had any pride in herself could be that self-effacing, for heaven's sake! To have to walk in your man's shadow and know that star-struck girls were always throwing themselves at him must be terrible.

Dismissing the idea from her mind with a mental shudder, Harry told the two men about her day at the studios, adding, 'This girl I'm working with, Emma Page, she comes from Birmingham and is staying at a hotel. She seems rather lonely and I wondered if we might offer her our spare room.'

Bob grinned. 'Feeling sorry for her, are you? Another stray that you want to take under your wing?'

'What's she like?' Eric asked.

'Very nice. A good sense of humour, and I think she could be a lot of fun.'

'No. I meant what does she look like?'

'Oh! Short and blonde. Cuddly.'

Eric looked pleased. Although he was so big himself, he much preferred short girls. 'You could try asking her over,' he suggested.

'All right. I'll ask her to supper one evening,' Harriet agreed. 'If you like her and she likes us, we'll offer her the room.'

At the studios the next morning, filming began in earnest and, after they'd got over their initial nervousness at working with a new director, both Julie and Harry responded well, but poor Emma kept forgetting to lower her voice and they had to do quite a few retakes, which made her even more nervous.

At the end of the day, Harriet invited her to go back to the house for a meal, but Emma shook her head dolefully. 'Thanks, but I don't think I'd better. I really feel that I ought to stay in and go over my lines for tomorrow again. I fluffed quite a few today.'

'Only because you got nervous. You were word-perfect when you started. Come home with me and have supper. You can stay the night and I'll drive you in in the morning.'

But Emma obstinately refused. 'No. This film is so important to me. I really must study my lines again and get an early night. I've got a scene with that American actress who's playing the murder victim tomorrow, and she's only over in England for a week, so I must get it right. If I waste the director's time again tomorrow he might decide to replace me.'

'I'm sure he wouldn't,' Harriet disagreed quickly. 'Look, Emma, you were picked out of hundreds of girls. You wouldn't have been chosen if the producers weren't absolutely sure you could play the part. You've just got to remember that you're not on a stage, that's all.'

In the end she persuaded Emma to come back with her, and she soon relaxed under the combined attentions of both Bob and Eric, who soon had her laughing. Towards the end of the evening Harry lifted an interrogative eyebrow at the two men and they both nodded approval, Eric most forcibly; so when Harriet took Emma up to show her the room she was to sleep in, she asked the other girl if she would care to stay with them for the duration of the film.

'Oh, I'd *love* to,' Emma said enthusiastically. 'As a matter of fact, I wanted to ask you if I could, but I thought you'd be sure to have lots of people wanting the room.'

'Not at the moment, so you're in luck. But you'll have to pay a quarter of the rent and do your share of the work,' Harry warned her.

'Oh, that's OK. I always had to help at home.'

As they drove into the studios the next morning, Harriet gave Emma all the tips she could. Whether it was that, or the fact that she wouldn't be by herself in the hotel any more, Emma was much more at ease and acted just as well as the others, much to her relief.

The days flew by with very little leisure time, and it came almost as a surprise when the director informed them that the star of the film had arrived in England and that they would be giving the party for Rex Kynaston the next day. He also told them that the Press had been invited, and they were all expected to attend as it would be a good opportunity to get publicity for the film.

'They would decide to hold the party on our day off,' Harry said in annoyance. 'Now I shall have to cancel a perfectly good date. And I bet you anything you like that they want a publicity picture of us fawning all over Rex Kynaston for the tabloids.'

Emma laughed. 'Well, that's one picture *I* won't mind having taken in the least.'

'Emma, if you let him see you drooling over him I shall disown you. How can you? He's nothing but a— but a blown-up image.'

'You don't know that,' Julie objected. 'He might just be everything he looks like on the screen. Big, beautiful, strong, capable . . . Mmm, I just can't wait to meet him.'

'And brainy, don't forget,' Harriet put in, ignoring the dreamy expression of Julie's eyes. 'In his television series he's supposed to be clever as well. And I bet you anything you like he isn't that, even if he's any of the other things.'

Julie's eyes narrowed. 'How much do you bet?'

Quite certain that she was right, Harriet said rashly, 'Anything you like. A hundred pounds.'

'Wow!' Both Julie and Emma looked taken aback and Julie shook her head. 'That's too steep for me. Why are you so certain?' she asked curiously.

'It just makes me angry, the way everybody drools over these plastic heroes,' Harry explained. 'Usually they're picked only for their looks and their physique. They have no acting training, and the expression on their faces never changes from the start of the programme to the end. If they were put in front of an audience they'd die a thousand deaths. In my opinion, they're just the male equivalent of the dumb blonde. And it makes me angry to think that there must be hundreds of good actors, who've taken the trouble to learn their craft, who can't get work just because they don't happen to be six feet four inches tall and exceptionally good-looking,' she finished vehemently.

Both Julie and Emma burst out laughing. 'Well, at least you've admitted that Rex Kynaston is exceptionally good-looking,' Julie pointed out. 'So that's one up to us. But I agree with you that it isn't fair,' she added, sobering. 'But that's just the way things are.'

'And if it comes to that, none of us would have got parts in this film if we hadn't been reasonably attractive,' Emma reminded them.

'But we're professional actresses; we've all been to drama school and done our stint in repertory theatre,' Harry pointed out. 'Whereas Rex Kynaston, for example, what training has he had? I read in a magazine that he'd been discovered working as a life-guard on a beach! And yet they're depending on *him* to make this film into a hit!' she said disgustedly.

'I see what you mean,' Emma agreed. But added hopefully, 'Maybe he'll turn out to be a natural actor.'

'Some hopes! The director will probably have to nurse him through every scene. You wait and see,' Harriet declared pessimistically. 'And another thing...' But then she hesitated, aware that she was about to indulge in gossip.

'What? What were you going to say?'

'Nothing. It doesn't matter.'

Julie looked at her sharply. 'If it's something about Rex Kynaston, I think you ought to tell us. After all, we've got to work with him, too,' she pointed out.

'Well, OK,' Harry agreed reluctantly. 'But don't spread it around. There's an actor who lives quite near me; his name is Michael Shelsher. Have you heard of him?'

Emma shook her head, but Julie said, 'Yes, I think I worked with him some years ago. A tall, very tough-looking man in his early thirties?'

'That's right,' Harry nodded. 'Well, he was in line to play the police detective in our film and was on the point of signing the contract, but Rex Kynaston has a clause in *his* contract giving him the right of veto over the rest of the cast, and he insisted on having someone else in the part—so Mike was out. And it hit poor Mike at a particularly bad time, too, because a play he'd been in hadn't made it to the West End. And he was also having trouble at home; his wife was pushing him to get an ordinary, steady job and he hoped this film would prove to her that he still had a future as an actor.'

'Did Rex Kynaston have something against Mike?' Julie asked.

'No. They'd never even met. Rex has never been to England before. It seems that he'd seen this other actor in a film, liked the look of him, and insisted on having him in the part.'

Emma gave her a horrified stare. 'You're not saying that Rex is *gay*, are you?'

Both Julie and Harry went into peals of laughter. 'No, of course not,' Harriet assured her. 'It was the man's *acting* he liked the look of.'

'From what I've heard, Rex Kynaston is quite the opposite,' Julie put in. 'He's supposed to have had an affair with almost every actress who's appeared in his series. I wonder if he'll make a play for one of us?'

The girls looked at each other, their faces sobering, and were silent with their own thoughts until Harry said slowly, 'I was in a film once—the flop I told you about—it had everything going for it until the producers decided to cast a big star in the lead. Or at least he *had* been a big star, but he was on the way out; all he was then was a big name. But he was hanging on for dear life and he insisted on virtually rewriting the script and having everything his own way, with the result that he completely ruined any chance the film had of being a success.' Harry paused, then added, 'He was on the way out sexually, too, but that didn't stop him from making life hell for every girl on the set. He seemed to think that just because he was a big star we would all be eager to jump into bed with him, even though he was nearly sixty and had had so many face-lifts he looked like a worn-out elevator.' Her voice grew bitter. 'He even used blackmail, threatening to get girls thrown out of the film if they didn't do what he wanted.' She was silent for a moment, her face withdrawn, but then she blinked and said, 'Of course, the film was a flop. The "big star" was never heard of again, but he had also harmed the careers of every other person associated with the film. So you can see why I'm against having Rex Kynaston in this film— he's already responsible for one actor losing a part, and if he starts throwing his weight around...'

She didn't have to say any more, the other two girls nodded in comprehension. 'Well, at least Rex isn't on his way out,' Emma said optimistically.

'No, but he's on his way up, which could be quite as bad,' Harry pointed out. But then her pessimistic mood suddenly broke, and she smiled. 'Well, at least we'll see him at the party and find out for ourselves just how much hold he has over the producers.'

'*And* if he's as big and gorgeous in real life as he is on the screen,' Emma added, putting on such a mock-lascivious look that they burst out laughing again.

So it was with mixed feelings of excited anticipation and apprehension that the three arrived at the London hotel where the party for Rex Kynaston was being held the next day. Harry, for all her reservations, knew that her career depended to a very large extent on publicity, and had dressed to look her best in a deep red-velvet dress that she knew was a perfect foil for her dark hair and creamy skin. It wasn't cut very low or anything like that—she detested pin-up pictures—but it had a scoop neckline that hinted at the swell of her breasts and it showed off the slimness of her tiny waist. However, it was her face and the beauty of her eyes that drew and held attention. Harriet knew that they were her best feature and years of experience had taught her just how to make them up to the very best advantage. And to use them, too. For television work especially, her eyes were her greatest asset, able to express every emotion without her saying a word.

Both Emma and Julie were aware of the value of publicity, too, and had dressed for the occasion, but in far more trendy clothes than Harry's. Emma wore a long shirt-shaped dress with a low sash and with a matching headband woven into her hair, which she'd done in a mass of tangled curls, and Julie was wearing a strapless, sequinned boob-tube with black harem trousers and very high-heeled shoes.

There were already quite a lot of Press people at the party when Harriet and Emma arrived, and they had to pose to have their photographs taken for a good couple of minutes before they were free to get themselves a drink and mingle with the guests. This was quite flattering, but both girls were realistic enough to know that the photographs might never appear; it usually depended on what space the editors had in their newspapers. Sometimes they were luckier with specialist film magazines, but there was a limit to how many photographs of up and coming young actresses, however beautiful, even these magazines would print.

Julie arrived late, but unfortunately didn't make the entrance she'd hoped for, as she was upstaged by the American actress playing the murder victim who arrived a minute later. As she had played opposite Rex Kynaston in an episode of his television series, she was instantly surrounded by the Press reporters who wanted her opinion of him.

'Is he really as good-looking as he appears on screen?' one of them asked her.

'Oh, definitely,' the actress gushed. 'And he has the most wonderful personality. 'And such a marvellous sense of humour. It was just great to work with him.'

'And was there any truth in the rumours that you two saw a lot of each other off the set, too?' someone asked.

The actress looked coy. 'You really shouldn't ask me that; I was married at the time, you know.'

A reporter seized his cue and said, 'Is the fact that you're not married now anything to do with Rex Kynaston?'

But after a trill of laughter, the actress would only say, 'Now that was naughty! Let's just say that we're looking forward to seeing each other again tonight. After all, what woman wouldn't look forward to seeing anybody as gorgeous as Rex?'

'Ugh!' After a few minutes of this, Harriet, who was standing within earshot, turned away in disgust and so missed the big moment that everyone had been waiting for.

The doors were thrown open and Rex Kynaston strolled rather than walked into the room. He was followed by an escort of about half a dozen men and a couple of women, all in full evening dress, although he himself was wearing a white tuxedo.

It was only when the people in the room broke into an involuntary ripple of applause that Harry realised he'd arrived and turned to look. The star of the picture was standing just inside the doorway, acknowledging his welcome with a wave and a big smile on his face; a face quite as handsome as it appeared on the screen, even though he still had the moustache that he wore in his television series. And the small screen had dwarfed him; in reality he seemed a giant compared to the men around him, standing taller than all of them and with a build to match. He went on smiling and nodding as everyone continued to applaud, his eyes working their way round the room until they reached Emma and Harry. Emma had a big, sloppy grin on her face and was clapping as enthusiastically as anyone, but Harry stood still, not seeing why she should applaud someone just because he happened to have been born with good looks. She was tall, too, and she saw the way that Rex Kynaston's eyes travelled over Emma and then came up to look at herself. He saw that she wasn't clapping and his dark eyes went to her face, meeting hers. Harry's chin came up in a cold, disapproving challenge for a moment, and then she quite deliberately turned her back on him as she went to get herself another drink.

The applause stopped soon after as the photographers rushed forward and flash bulbs popped for several minutes among shouts of, 'This way, Rex!' and 'Over here, Rex.' And then the American actress went forward to hug and kiss him, so the bulbs started flashing all over again. Bored, Harriet wandered to the back of the room to look at all the food laid out on the long buffet tables. The film company had really gone to town and there was a beautiful spread, everything from smoked salmon to caviar. What a waste for someone like Rex Kynaston, Harriet thought cynically. But no, that wasn't fair; this party was only an excuse to get publicity for the picture, and the food was for the benefit of the Press as much as anyone. It was only by their good offices that the film would get the publicity and, hopefully, good reviews when it was finished and had its preview in the cinema.

The producer had moved to a microphone and was making a speech of welcome, so Harriet turned and listened politely. Then it was Rex Kynaston's turn. He gave everyone that charmingly boyish smile again, his eyes crinkling at the corners, and then mouthed the usual platitudes about how pleased he was to be here, how much he was looking forward to making the film and seeing more of this delightful country. He had an attractive voice, Harriet had to admit that, as she listened with her actress's trained ear; it was deep and resonant and without too much of an American drawl. In fact, his accent wasn't so much American as mid-Atlantic, one that could be easily understood by both countries.

Harriet liked good voices, and it rather annoyed her that Rex Kynaston had such an attractive one. Still, it would make the scenes she had to play with him that much easier, although it would have been better if she could have shut her eyes and cut out the rest of him!

'Harry, you've just got to admit that he's gorgeous!' Emma came rushing up to her the minute Rex's speech was over. 'Isn't it exciting? I can't wait till we start filming on Monday. If there's time I might even get to play a small scene with him.'

Harry smiled at Emma, but refused to admit that she was secretly rather impressed by Rex's looks. She was still willing to take a bet that he couldn't act.

The star was now being introduced to the film's backers, the company's stills photographer taking a record of each handshake for posterity. Soon someone came over to the two girls and said, 'The director would like you to come over and meet Mr Kynaston now, girls.'

A director's request was a command and they dutifully made their way across the room, Emma impatiently rushing ahead. Julie was already there, and was having her picture taken holding on to Rex's arm and looking up at him admiringly. Harriet stood back as Emma was introduced; Rex gave her one of his famous smiles, having to stoop quite low as he said, 'Hi there, Emma, pleased to be working with you.'

'And this,' the director said jovially, as he put a hand under Harry's elbow and drew her forward, 'is the third of our trio of young starlets, Harriet Sutton.'

There was an instant look of recognition in Rex's eyes as he greeted her, followed by one of speculation. 'Well, hello there, Harriet,' he said, extending his hand. 'Great to meet you.'

'How do you do, Mr Kynaston?' Harriet returned, her eyes cool. Her hand was taken in a firm grip, but she quickly disengaged it.

A flash bulb went off in her face and then one of the photographers called, 'How about a picture of you with the three girls, Rex?'

'Sure, happy to oblige.' He spread his arms to take in the three of them, but Harry adroitly let Emma come between them so that she was on the outside. They all smiled dutifully for the cameras, and then someone suggested that Rex sit down and the girls pose round him. She let Emma and Julie sit on his knees, but had to lean over his shoulder, with her head close to his, the American actress coming into the picture on the other side. The lights flashed again and then, quite unexpectedly, Rex turned his head to look challengingly into Harry's eyes—and kissed her!

Harry recoiled as if she'd been stung, and for a moment his dark eyes laughed at her, but then Rex turned to kiss the American actress and then Julie and Emma. All the kisses were snapped eagerly, of course, by the grinning photographers!

Stepping quickly away, her cheeks flushed with annoyance, Harry went to talk to someone she knew at the other side of the room, leaving the other girls to stay clustered around Rex, hanging on to his every word. But presently the group broke up as everyone moved over to the tables to help themselves to the food.

'What do you think of him now, Harry?' Julie demanded as she and Emma joined her. 'You've got to admit that he's every bit as sexy as he appears on the screen.'

Harriet shrugged. 'I'm not going to draw any conclusions until I've seen him act—or try to'

Julie laughed. 'That's an opinion in itself. Why did you go away after the photographs? You should have stayed and talked. He was really interesting.'

'Really?' Harriet asked disbelievingly. 'What did he talk about—himself?'

'Well, yes, I suppose he did,' Emma admitted. 'But only because we asked him. It was about his television series mostly. He was telling us that the episodes we're seeing in England are at least six months behind those they're showing in America.'

Harry laughed teasingly. 'I'm surprised you can tell the difference. They're all virtually the same. When you've seen one programme in Rex Kynaston's series, you've seen the lot!'

Emma began to laugh, but then stopped abruptly, her face looking dismayed as she looked past Harriet. 'Oh, how ridiculous,' she said quickly. 'Who said that to you? It must have been a complete idiot.'

Frowning in puzzlement, Harry was about to deny that anyone had said it to her, but Julie purposely trod on her toe and she realised at last that someone was standing behind her, listening. And from the admiring smile on Emma's face and the way she was tilting her head to look very high, it just had to be Rex Kynaston.

So Harry, instead of trying to cover her *faux pas*, added, 'I would hardly call the person who told me an idiot; it was a very discerning television critic.'

'Well, everyone's entitled to their opinion,' a deep voice said behind her and she turned to see Rex standing close by, a glass of champagne in his hand. His eyes rested for a moment on Harriet's face, and she had the strange feeling that he knew exactly what she thought of him, and that he found it rather amusing. But then he looked away and said, 'That food sure looks good. Aren't you girls eating?' He smiled at Julie. 'How about filling up a plate for me while you're getting yours?'

'Why, of course!' Julie looked quite flattered at being treated like a waitress. 'What do you like?'

'Oh, just anything will be fine.'

Julie went to push her way through the crowd of people at the buffet and Rex smiled at Emma. 'What part do you play in the film?'

'Oh, I haven't got a very big part. It's my first film, you see. But I appear in the very first scene we're going to shoot with you, when you come to call at the flat. I have to open the door to you in my dressing-gown and slippers.'

'That's right, I remember.' Rex smiled at her. 'Are you a comedy actress?'

The question pleased Emma, who rather fancied herself in comedy, and she started telling him about some of the roles she'd played in the past. Harry stood quietly by, unable to move away because she was trapped between the wall and a table, and wondered if Rex Kynaston ever stopped smiling. He couldn't find the world that good, surely? But maybe he did, the way every female in the place was fawning on him. She and Emma were the focus of many envious eyes as he stood listening and nodding, apparently giving Emma all his attention.

But maybe he wasn't, because as soon as Emma paused for breath he turned to Harriet and said, 'And what part do you play—Harriet, isn't it? That's a pretty name.'

'Oh, but we all call her Harry,' Emma told him before she could open her mouth. 'Everyone does. She plays the part of Nicky Wells.'

'Nicky Wells? Oh, yes, I remember.' Again he gave her a mockingly speculative look that Harriet found exceedingly annoying, but he merely glanced down at his glass and said to Emma, 'Hey, our glasses are empty.

How about using your charms on one of the waiters and rustling up a bottle of champagne for us?'

Emma giggled. 'All right, I'll try. I'll tell him it's for you.'

'Tell him it's for you, and he'll probably give you two,' Rex corrected her, again bringing the crinkly-eyed smile into play.

Realising that she was going to be left alone with Rex, Harry went to move past him to follow Emma, but he took a pace forward and barred her way. Harriet stood still for a moment, then slowly lifted her head to look at him. She had to lift it an awfully long way. A mocking smile played around his lips as Rex said softly, 'You know, I get the impression that you disapprove of me, Harry.'

Harriet's eyes widened; she hadn't suspected that he would be so acute, and she was rather annoyed with herself. No way had she wanted to draw his attention to her. And what a poser to have to answer! If she denied it she would flatter his already enlarged ego, and if she agreed then he could make life extremely difficult for her on the set. It was obvious that Rex recognised the quandary he had set for her, because there was a distinctly malicious look of enjoyment in his eyes.

'Isn't that so?' he demanded.

She was about to make some kind of extemporary answer when, to her profound relief, the American actress saw that they were alone and came over to join them, linking her arm familiarly through Rex's. 'It's so long since I've seen you,' she pouted. 'Don't you ever return calls?'

'I've been pretty busy,' Rex told her.

The actress tried to pull him away from Harry, but trying to move Rex Kynaston when he wanted to stay put was like trying to move a solid rock. Lifting up a hand, he signalled to a member of the production company who was hovering nearby. 'Say, how about taking this young lady to get some food?'

For a moment the actress looked startled and then angry, but she had more sense than to make a scene, and merely shot Rex a malevolent look before going off with her more than willing escort. Harriet took the opportunity to slip past, but she had only taken a couple of steps before Rex put a firm hand under her elbow and brought her to a halt. 'You haven't answered my question,' he reminded her.

He looked down at her, so physically large that he overwhelmed her. So arrantly masculine that she couldn't help but be aware of him. And so sure of his almighty attraction to women that he made her suddenly very angry. Throwing caution to the winds, she answered impetuously, 'All right, since you insist. Yes, I do disapprove of you.' She expected him to be angry, or at the least to walk away, but he merely raised a sardonic, amused eyebrow. Goaded into an unusual fit of temper by his mockery, she added rashly, 'In fact, I'd go further than that, and say that I haven't yet seen anything of you that's at all likeable, if you really want to know.'

To her annoyance, Rex merely grinned widely. 'In that case,' he said silkily, 'that love scene we're going to do together should turn out to be a very interesting experience, shouldn't it?'

CHAPTER TWO

HARRIET looked at Rex with startled eyes; she had forgotten all about having to work with him when she had made that angry retort. She groaned inwardly, wishing that she had dissembled, but it was too late now. Drawing herself up, her hazel eyes cold as chips of green ice on stone, she merely gazed disdainfully at his taunting face.

'Brrr!' Rex pretended to shiver theatrically. 'I heard that you English girls were cold, and now I know what they mean. Are you always this glacial?'

Almost as if to belie his words, Emma came rushing up at that moment, laughing and clutching a bottle of champagne. 'Here we are! Let's have your glasses.' She filled them up and held one out to Rex. He took it and moved to help Julie who was trying to reach them with two large plates full of food.

'I've got enough for all of us,' she announced triumphantly.

However, after picking at a couple of canapés, Rex didn't seem to be interested in the food any more. Someone greeted him, and he moved away a little to talk and then began to circulate around the room. But before he did so Harriet felt his eyes on her and was compelled to look up. For several seconds she fought the compulsion, but eventually had to lift her head and look at him. His dark eyes met her cold glance triumphantly, and he lifted his glass in a gesture that was in itself a form of challenge, taking a long drink, his eyes holding hers the whole time.

It was a physical effort to tear her eyes away, and to her annoynace Harry found that her heart was beating too fast and too loud. Damn the man! Out of the whole roomful of people, why did he have to pick on her as the butt of his chauvinistic ego? But then she had to admit that she had probably made her disapproval plain enough and, to a man as conceited as Rex evidently was, even aloofness would act as a challenge; he just had to have every woman he came in contact with yapping round his heels like a pet dog. And he was obviously used to handling his fans; look at the way he had sent Julie and Emma running to do his bidding, and the way he had got rid of the American actress when he didn't want her around. And he hadn't wanted her around because he had wanted to be alone with Harriet. For a moment she had the feeling that she was getting out of her depth, but then shook it off. He had just been amused to find someone who didn't throw herself at him like all the others, that was all. He might be a bit vindictive to her on the set and make sure that he upstaged her, but he would soon forget all about her when he started dating some of the better-known actresses who were bound to want to be seen out with him.

With this comforting thought, Harriet was able to start enjoying the party, especially as Rex left about an hour afterwards, using jet-lag as an excuse; although anyone who looked less jet-lagged, Harriet had yet to see.

After the star had gone, the champagne seemed to suddenly run out, so the Press immediately left *en masse* and the party broke up soon afterwards.

Harry and Emma drove home together, with Emma excitedly talking about Rex all the way. 'I do hope I get to play that part with him on Monday,' she said for the fifth time. 'I know that that scene is supposed to be a funny one where I open the door to him with cream on my face and everything, but I don't see why I shouldn't be wearing quite a sexy nightdress instead of a dressing-gown, do you? As a matter of fact I have one of my own I could take along, and a pair of black mink mules to match.'

'Where on earth did you find black mink mules?' Harriet demanded.

'What? Oh, they were a present. From—er—someone I know back in Birmingham.'

Guessing that the 'someone' was a man, Harry refrained from asking any more questions. She was tolerant towards other people's morals; being in a house with two men who often brought girls home, she didn't have much choice, really. And the last girl who'd lived there had brought her boyfriend back so often that they had threatened to charge him rent, so the two had found a flat and gone to live together, which was why there had been an empty room for Emma.

On Sunday she drove to her family home and spent the day helping her brothers to restore an old MG sports car, lovingly rubbing down the bodywork ready for re-painting. It was quite tiring physical work, but Harriet was young and strong and she was up the next morning in time to haul Emma out of bed so that they were at the studios by seven-thirty, ready to be made-up.

The first scenes to be shot that morning were with actors taking the parts of police officers investigating the murder, and it wasn't until the afternoon that Rex

Kynaston came on to the set to shoot his first scenes, again with the police officer actors. They were all keen to see how well—or how badly—he would act, so it was with some disappointment that the girls had to go to a local hall that had been hired by the film company as a rehearsal room, to go over some scenes they would be playing together the next day.

Then they had to go back to the studios for Emma to get ready for her scene with Rex. Emma was a mixture of emotions, a cross between excited and nervous, which made her a bit giggly. 'You will come on the set with me, won't you?' she appealed to Harriet. 'I shall need some moral support.'

'I wouldn't miss it for worlds. I'd really like to see Rex Kynaston make a fool of himself after the way he behaved at the party. How about you, Julie?'

But Julie shook her head. 'I'd rather get home. But promise to tell me all about it tomorrow.'

So they split up; Julie to go home, Emma to go on to the set and Harry to creep quietly into the studio and lean against the wall to watch. There was the usual delay while the technicians hurried round getting the lighting right and the cameramen worked out their distances, while the director took Rex aside and told him what he wanted.

'OK, we'll run it through,' the director ordered.

The scene was set in the corridor leading up to the front door of the murdered girl's flat. All Rex had to do was to walk up to the door, ring the bell, and Emma would answer it. They would then hold a short conversation and she was to let him in. Harriet almost burst out laughing when Emma opened the door. Not only had the director not allowed her to wear her sexy nightdress and mules, but he had made her put half her hair in rollers, the other half hanging wetly at the side of her head. There was an indignant look in Emma's eyes that had nothing to do with acting, and Harry guessed that she must really be hating having to play her first scene with a star like Rex, looking like a clown. They went through the action three times, with Emma fluffing her lines each time and getting more uptight by the minute. The director was sympathetic, but he had his shooting schedule and the enormous expense of the production to think of, and began to get a little impatient. Also, it was the end of the day and everyone wanted to go home. Harry's heart went out to Emma, but there was nothing she could do except keep her fingers crossed and hope that the other girl would soon relax. They tried it again for a fourth time, and again Emma got it wrong after a couple of sentences.

'OK, let's do it once more. Just try and take it easy, Emma. You're doing fine,' the director encouraged.

But Emma knew she wasn't and turned away with a doleful face. It didn't go right this time either, but it wasn't Emma's fault. When she opened the door after Rex's ring, her eyes widened and she burst into a fit of laughter.

'What the...?' the director began, and then he and all the crew broke into laughter, too. From somewhere, Rex had found a pair of fanglike teeth that they used in vampire films, and had opened his mouth to reveal them just as Emma had begun to speak. He stood there, grinning round at them all, and even Harry had to smile; the teeth looked so wrong in his handsome face.

Emma laughed so much that she had to have her make-up repaired, but Rex's ruse worked, because she did the next take perfectly, completely relaxed.

'OK, it's a wrap,' the director declared, and everyone gave a great sight of relief, glad that the day was over. Emma ran to get changed and have her hair dried, afraid of catching a cold.

As she couldn't go home without her, Harry stayed on the set, watching as the technicians covered the cameras and switched off the huge lights. She had appeared in many television shows before, but only one feature film, so it was interesting to watch the way the technicians worked. Rex had left the set with the director, and she supposed that he was being escorted to his luxury dressing-room just off the set. She had to admit that the joke he'd played to put Emma at ease had surprised her considerably; she hadn't expected him to be the kind of man who would bother about the feelings of his fellow actors. But maybe he was used to playing opposite young starlets who were in awe of him, and had used this method before to make them relax. His acting, too, had somewhat surprised her; he had used the set and said his lines quite naturally. But it was an easy scene, anyone could have done it, she thought disparagingly.

She walked over to the set of the living-room, where she would have to act out a scene opposite Rex tomorrow. There were only ordinary lights on now, no great flood-lights to chase the shadows away and make it seem like daylight. Looking round the set, it came to Harriet that she might have done Rex an injustice. He was American, a foreigner, for all they spoke the same language—or near enough—among a crew and cast of British people.

The only other 'foreigner' was the American actress, but she wasn't playing opposite him. It could have made him nervous and tense, too, like Emma, but it was he who had put the English girl at ease.

Harriet wondered if *she* would be nervous when she acted with him, and fervently hoped she wouldn't be. She prided herself on her professional attitude to her work, and always made sure that she knew exactly what she was supposed to be doing as far as she could. There were always unknown factors, of course, like the technicians' requirements and any changes the director or screen-writers might want to make, but, allowing for these, Harry tried to be as familiar as she could with what she had to do.

Going over tomorrow's scene in her mind, she began to move around the set, murmuring her lines under her breath, working out how she was going to act them, and concentrating so intently that she didn't realise that someone had come on to the set and was watching her, until she came to the end of the scene. She nodded, satisfied that she knew her lines correctly, and looked up. Rex was standing in the shadow thrown by one of the false walls of the set. When he saw that she'd seen him, he moved forward and came to stand beside her.

'Tomorrow's scene?' he asked, raising an eyebrow.

'Yes,' Harry admitted reluctantly, feeling that she had somehow given him the edge on her. So she added quickly, 'It was just something to do while I waited for Emma.'

She thought she saw a swift gleam of amusement in his eyes, but he merely said, 'Are you and she friends?'

'Not really. We only met on the set just over a week ago. But Emma has taken a room in the house where I live.' Harry stopped, realising that she was talking to cover up her embarrassment.

'So you travel to the studios together?' Rex pursued.

'Yes.'

'In the company limo?'

For a second she didn't understand, but then gave rather a grim smile and shook her head. 'Oh, no! Emma and I aren't important enough to rate a car from the film company. I have my own transport.'

His eyes had flickered with interest at her tone, but Rex didn't follow it up, instead asking, 'Where do you travel to? London?'

She nodded rather warily. 'Yes.'

'I'm staying in London, too. At a flat in Kensington. Northrop Building. Do you know it?'

Harriet certainly did. It wasn't that far from where she lived. But, 'I've heard of it,' was all she would admit to.

'The company aren't putting you up there?'

She laughed shortly. 'You have strange ideas about British film companies. You're the only one who is being put up in a flat. Oh, except the other American actress, of course. But she's finished her part now, so it's just you. We unknown mortals have to make our way here under our own steam from our own homes every day.'

There was a definite dig in her tone, but either Rex was very obtuse or he chose to ignore it. 'This is my first trip to England,' he told her. 'London looks an interesting city, but I could sure use a guide.'

He paused suggestively and Harry supposed that he expected her to jump to offer herself, but if so he was disappointed because she immediately said shortly, 'I'm quite sure the film company would be happy to provide you with one.'

Rex's lips curled into a wry smile. 'Maybe you could tell me some places I should go see.'

Harriet shrugged as she walked off the set. 'There are hundreds of places. Any tourist centre will give you all the information you want. I think I'll go and see what's keeping Emma.'

'Harry!' Rex's sharp voice echoed in the empty studio, bringing her to a stop. Slowly she turned to face him. His tall frame cast a long shadow that reached to her feet as he stood looking at her. 'Do you always treat visitors to your country like this?' he demanded. 'Don't you like Americans or something? Or is it just me?'

Slowly she answered, 'I have no reason to dislike Americans.'

Rex moved towards her, his shadow gradually engulfing her until he stood quite close, his eyes fixed on her face. 'And do you have any reason to dislike me?'

His dark eyes held hers for a long moment, but then Harry turned on her heel, reluctant to answer such a loaded question. 'There are several very good museums quite close to where you're staying,' she told him, speaking quickly so that he couldn't interrupt. 'The British Museum, for example, contains the famous Elgin Marbles from the Parthenon in Athens. And I think there are a few pavement artists still left who gather there.'

'Pavement artists?' Rex asked with a frown of puzzlement.

'Yes. You know, people who draw pictures in chalk on the pavement.'

He shook his head. 'I'm sorry, but what's a pavement?'

'Oh! Well, a pavement is the thing you walk on at the side of the road.'

His face cleared. 'You mean a sidewalk.'

'Do I? Yes, I suppose I do, if that's what you call it in America.'

Rex gave one of his famous smiles. 'Who was it said that we're two countries divided by a common language?'

'*And* a very large ocean,' Harriet reminded him, her face softening a little.

'That's true enough.' His voice became persuasive. 'London can be a big and lonely place when you're a stranger and don't know anyone.'

But Harry wasn't going to let him make her feel sorry for him. 'My heart bleeds for you,' she answered mockingly.

He grinned. 'Do you have a heart, Harry?' She didn't answer so he said, 'If you had, you'd take pity on me and at least have a drink with me while you tell me what other places I could visit.'

'I can't,' she said at once. 'I told you, I'm going home with Emma.'

'I meant Emma too, of course,' he said smoothly, and turned as they heard footsteps. 'And here she is. We were just talking about you,' he told Emma, as soon as she came close enough.

'Oh, really? What about me?' she asked, eager and flattered.

'We were arranging for me to take you both out for a drink tonight, but Harry wasn't sure whether you would feel up to it.'

Emma shot Harriet an angry look. 'Of course I am. I'd love to come,' she added, with a melting smile for Rex.

But all he got from Harry was a glare for the way he'd twisted everything. 'In that case, I'm sure you'll be able to manage quite well without me. I have several things to do at home.'

'But you promised to tell me about all the places I should see in London,' Rex reminded her audaciously.

'I don't remember making any promise,' she argued challengingly. 'And I don't remember saying I would go for a drink.'

'That's OK,' Emma interrupted. 'I can tell you what to see, if Harry's tired.'

Rex looked at Harriet over the top of Emma's head, almost as if the other girl wasn't there. His dark eyes held hers, and she felt suddenly as if she was being dared to do something she was half afraid of. Her heart began to beat rather fast and she felt a strange tightening sensation in her chest as Rex said softly, 'Are you tired, Harry?'

Her chin came up defiantly, her cool eyes betraying nothing of her inner feelings. 'No, I'm not tired,' she said firmly. 'But I...'

'Great!' Rex broke in. 'So we'll go to one of those quaint old English pubs I'm always hearing about, and you two can tell me about all the places I should go to. My driver's waiting outside, so we'll go in my car.'

Harriet gave him an indignant glare, aware that he had again manoeuvred her into getting his own way. 'Sorry,' she snapped. 'But I have my own car, and if I don't take it, we won't be able to get to work tomorrow.'

'OK, so we'll all go in your car,' Rex returned, in no way put out.

Both Emma and Harry laughed. 'Mine is only a two-seater,' Harriet explained. 'So you and Emma can go ahead and I'll follow.'

Rex gave her a shrewd look and she had the uncomfortable feeling that he'd guessed her intention to get 'lost' on the way. 'No, you're familiar with the area. We'll follow you.'

So she had no choice but to drive ahead of Rex's big chauffeur-driven company car to a pub only a short distance from her own home and Rex's flat. After he'd dropped them off, the driver went home, Rex telling him that he would take a cab when he was ready to go back to the flat. The pub, The Red Lion, looked very ordinary from the outside, but inside it still had all the etched glass and shining brass fittings from its original Victorian days. The atmosphere was warm and friendly, making it a place in which you immediately felt welcome and at ease.

Rex looked round appreciatively. 'They've got a copy of a British pub at the Epcot Centre in Florida,' he told them, 'but it isn't like this.'

'That's because this is the genuine article,' Emma said unnecessarily, excited at being seen out with him.

'I sure wish we had this back home,' Rex commented with enthusiasm.

'Why don't you buy it and take it back with you?' Harriet suggested flippantly. 'You could put it on the shore beside London Bridge and the *Queen Mary*.'

Rex grinned, in no way put out. 'That's quite a sharp tongue you have there, Harry. I wonder why you like cutting me with it?'

Harriet flushed slightly, acknowledging the hit, but was perversely angry with him because he hadn't got annoyed with *her*. He must be so thick-skinned and ego-tistical that he can't believe that there's someone who just doesn't like him, she thought irritably. She went to sit at a marble-topped, cast-iron table while Rex went to the bar to get their drinks. Emma went with him in case he needed any help sorting out the unfamiliar currency. When they came back, he politely waited for Emma to sit down on Harriet's left and then, to Emma's chagrin, he sat down on the other side, so that Harry was between them.

'Are all English pubs like this?' he asked her.

'No. This is a particularly good one. But this is a London pub; the country pubs in small villages are quite different.'

'You'll have to take me to one of those, then,' he said, and she wished she'd kept her mouth shut. But she had her revenge a moment later when he took a drink of the pint mug of beer in front of him and his face glazed over. 'My God, this beer is *warm*!'

Harry's eyes danced with laughter. 'Well, of course it is. That's *real* ale. The original brew. The British don't like their drinks half-filled with crushed ice, or their beer so cold and gassy that the bubbles freeze in their throats.'

He shot her a look under his brows, but Rex took another, more cautious sip. 'It's going to take some getting used to.'

'Why don't you have something else?' Emma suggested. 'A cocktail, or gin, or something with ice in it?'

Shaking his handsome head, Rex said, 'No, I guess I'll stick with this.' Looking at Harriet he said, 'Have you ever been to America?'

'Yes. Once.'

He looked at her, holding her eyes. 'It was a pity you didn't have someone you knew there. Someone who could have taken you round and shown you what America is like. How beautiful it can be. But then, I guess that's what every stranger to a country needs, someone to show them around.'

The message came across loud and clear, but Harry didn't take it up, instead leaving it to Emma to offer herself. But to her surprise the other girl didn't say anything, and when Harry glanced at her she saw that Emma was looking from one to the other of them and then down at her drink.

For some unknown reason, Harriet immediately felt guilty and she said quickly, 'We can give you a list of places to go to, can't we, Emma? There's the Tower of London, and Trafalgar Square, and then there's the Changing of the Guard at Buckingham Palace, you must see that. Where else can you think of, Emma?'

The other girl joined in, and Harriet made sure that the conversation stayed general, often not answering a question of Rex's to make sure that Emma wasn't shut out again. At one point she sat back in her seat while the other two were talking, looking round the pub that had begun to fill up now. The air was a little smoky and the talk and laughter louder, and she noticed that a great many sidelong looks were coming in their direction. It was Harry's local pub, the nearest one to her home, and she had been there lots of times with Bob and Eric, so she knew a lot of the regulars. As an actress, she was something of a minor celebrity, and they all recognised Rex, of course, from his television show; but British people were basically polite and wouldn't dream of invading their privacy to ask for autographs in a place like this. There were some speculative glances coming her and Emma's way too, and she could almost hear the brains ticking over, wondering who they were and whether Rex intended taking one or both of them to bed. Having two good-looking girls with him must be pushing up his stock considerably. But then they probably expected that from the kind of hero he portrayed on the small screen.

The thought made her lips curve and she looked back at the others, to find Rex watching her, his eyes fixed intently on her face. He smiled at her, his eyes holding hers, not the big smile that he used as an actor and a personality, but a small, private smile that was warm and friendly, that shut out everyone else in the room. Slowly, almost against her will, Harry found herself smiling back, her face transformed into beauty.

Rex became very still, as if his whole being was suspended in time as he looked at her with rapt attention. Then he let out his breath on a long sigh and blinked as if he'd been miles away. 'Hey—er—how about another drink?'

Harry stood up. 'Our round. I'll get them.'

But Rex immediately got to his feet and put his hand on her arm to stop her. 'No way. Not when you're with me.'

He squeezed her arm a little, but Harry merely nodded and said, 'Thanks,' then sat down again.

Emma let him go up to the bar by himself this time, and the two girls watched as the landlord started chatting to him, and other people sitting at the bar joined in. 'Do you think we ought to rescue him?' Emma asked.

Harry shook her head with a laugh. 'I'm quite sure Rex is big and capable enough to...' Her voice broke off and she gave a little exclamation of dismay. 'Oh, no!'

'What is it? What's the matter?' Emma followed her gaze, but could see nothing extraordinary.

'You see that man who's just come into the other bar? The tall one with fair hair?' The man in question looked in their direction as she spoke, and Harry hastily lifted her arm up to her hair, trying to hide her face.

'Yes. What about him? Who is he? I've never seen him before.'

'You remember the actor I told you about—the one who landed a part in our film until Rex said he wanted someone else?'

Emma's eyes widened. 'It isn't him?'

'It most certainly is—Mike Shelsher. Oh, lord, I hope he doesn't see me. He's bound to come over if he does.'

She kept her head turned away and it looked as if she was going to be lucky, because Emma reported that he had his back to them and was walking away. But just then there was a loud burst of laughter at the bar, where Rex had cracked a joke, and Mike Shelsher looked across from his bar to their own and saw him.

Harriet got nervously to her feet as Rex carried the drinks over and put them on the table. 'I—er—it's getting awfully late. Perhaps we ought to go.'

'Go? I thought you wanted another drink?'

'We're not thirsty. I really think we ought to...'

But it was too late. The thwarted actor had come into their bar and was standing in the doorway, glowering across at them. There was a pinched, mean look about his mouth, and he swayed a little on his feet, making Harry realise with dismay that he had already had quite a lot to drink. Coming up behind Rex he said belligerently, 'Well, well, well! If it isn't the big star himself.'

Rex looked into Harry's anxious face and slowly straightened up to turn round and face the other man.

'Oh, hello, Mike,' Harry said hollowly. 'We were just leaving.'

'Doesn't look like it to me,' Mike returned, looking at the drinks on the table.

'You're right, we're not,' Rex put in firmly. He glanced at Harry. 'Friend of yours?'

'Er—yes. This is Michael Shelsher. Mike, this is . . .'

'Oh, there's no need to tell me who he is,' Mike interrupted in heavy sarcasm. 'Everyone knows Rex Kynaston—the next step down from God Almighty!'

The vehement hatred in his tone created a small, stunned silence into which Harry said, 'Actually I was going to introduce you to Emma Page, who's sharing the house with us for a few months.'

Emma immediately picked up her cue and gave Mike a winning smile. 'Hello, Mike, nice to meet you. Do you live round here?'

But their attempts to diffuse the tension were completely useless; Mike ignored them and glared belligerently at Rex. The two men drew themselves up to their full heights as they sized each other up, Rex warily, Mike obviously spoiling for a fight. They were both big and broad men, but Mike had started to let himself go and it showed in the heaviness of his jaw and the thickening of his waistline, whereas Rex was lean and hard, his body honed to the peak of fitness by constant exercise. As they faced each other, feet apart, their shoulders slightly hunched, Harry was reminded vividly of two powerful primitive animals about to battle for supremacy, and a cold shiver of fear ran through her. Feeling that she just couldn't let this happen, she stepped quickly between them and faced Mike. 'Please,' she said urgently, 'I'm sure there's been a misunderstanding. I'm sure Rex wouldn't have...'

'There's no bloody misunderstanding,' Mike cut in aggressively. 'That jumped up beach boy did me out of the best part I've been offered in years.'

'Just who is this guy?' Rex demanded behind her.

Harry turned and gave him a cold look, aware of how justified Mike was in being so angry. 'Mike is an actor. He was offered the part of the police detective in the film, but the offer was withdrawn when you decided that you wanted someone else in the role. Naturally he's—rather annoyed.'

Rex gave her a derisive look but, before he could say anything, Mike said savagely, 'I'm more than bloody annoyed—I'm going to smash his face so hard he won't be taking part in anything for months!'

He took a determined step forward, his fists rising, but Harry stayed where she was and said to Rex, 'Get out of here, quickly.'

'I'm not afraid of him.'

'Don't be stupid,' she told him tersely. 'He means it. He'll use your head like a punchbag if you don't get out.'

But Rex only gave her a scornful look and stayed where he was.

'Get out of the way, Harry.' Mike tried to push her aside, but she put her hands up to stop him.

'Mike, *please*! Think what could happen. You could be arrested and put in prison. Then what would your wife do?'

'She wouldn't even know about it. She's left me. And all because of this bastard!' And he took a lunge at Rex over Harry's shoulder.

'Hold hard!' The landlord came rushing up, afraid of seeing his bar turned into a battleground. 'If you two are going to fight, then you can do it outside.' And he tried to grab Mike's arm.

But Mike suddenly exploded with rage and pushed the poor landlord across the room, knocking down a table as he did so. Then he went for Rex, charging at him like a maddened bull.

Harry was still in front of Rex and stood rooted in fear and consternation, expecting to be thrown aside too, but Rex grabbed her arm and pulled her out of the way, which left him wide open to a savage blow from Mike which landed on the side of his jaw. Rex staggered backwards, but somehow managed to stay on his feet and lift up his arms to defend himself against the barrage of punches that Mike aimed at his head. Harry and Emma could only stand by, clutching each other and watching in horrified disbelief, expecting Rex to be knocked to the ground and beaten up. But suddenly Rex regained his balance and everything changed. One minute Mike had the upper hand, the next Rex had grabbed his arm and twisted it behind him, forcing Mike to his knees, his face twisting in surprise more than pain.

'Christ, let go! You'll break my arm,' Mike yelled out.

Rex stood over him, breathing heavily, his clothes dishevelled and a lock of dark hair falling over his forehead. 'I *ought* to break your damn arm!' he said angrily, but then gave Mike a push that sent him sprawling on his face on the carpet. 'Get out of here before I change my mind,' he growled in disgust.

The landlord and another man came forward to help Mike to his feet, but he seemed so stunned by his easy defeat that he had no fight left in him. 'I've got my car outside. I'll take him home,' the man offered.

When they'd gone, there was a short silence in the bar, then someone gave a spontaneous cheer and soon nearly everyone was joining in. Rex grinned and raised a hand in acknowledgement as he pushed his hair back from his forehead. But there was no humour in his eyes as he turned to the two girls and said, 'Let's get out of here.'

They followed him outside, Harry still feeling shaken and infinitely relieved that it hadn't developed into an all-out brawl—thanks to Rex. He must be immensely powerful to overcome a man as big as Mike so easily. For a while there she had really been afraid that Mike would beat up Rex's face as he'd threatened. And heaven knows what would have happened to the film then, if Rex was unable to play his part. As they reached the corner, Rex came to a halt, and she turned to him to apologise and to thank him for not hitting Mike back as he so easily could have done, but before she could speak he said abruptly, 'Have you got your car keys?'

'Why, yes.'

Harriet got them out of her bag, but to her surprise Rex took them from her and gave them to Emma. 'Wait in the car, will you, honey?' he said to her. Then he turned to Harry, his face and voice cold as he said, 'I want to talk to you—alone.'

'Harry?' Emma said uncertainly, looking from one to the other.

'I—er—it's all right, Emma. I won't be a moment,' Harry answered, wondering uneasily what was coming.

She waited until Emma was out of sight and said, 'What do you want?'

Leaning forward, Rex caught hold of her wrist in a tight grip, his eyes like drops of arctic ice. 'As if you didn't know,' he said scathingly.

'I—I don't. Unless it's about Mike.'

'You bet your sweet life it's about Mike!' Rex snarled. 'I want to know just why you set me up back there. Why you dislike me so much that you led me straight into a fight where you expected me to get beaten to a pulp!'

CHAPTER THREE

'But—but I didn't,' Harriet protested in consternation. 'I didn't know he was going to be there.'

'Like hell!' Rex said in disgust. 'Do you really expect me to believe that it was a coincidence? You take me to the one pub in London where the one man in England who thinks he has a reason to hate my guts just happens to walk in! Oh, no, I'm not buying that.'

'But it's true! Look, the pub is the nearest one to where I live, and Mike is a neighbour, so it's his nearest one, too. He goes in there a lot.'

'And, knowing that, you decided to take me there.'

Harry flushed. 'I was going to apologise to you about that. I should have remembered. But when you said you wanted to go to a pub, I just naturally thought of this one.'

Rex gave her a look of total disbelief. 'You made it plain that you'd got something against me right from the beginning, and now I know what it is. You're on that guy's side. You made that more than obvious back there in the pub.'

Her chin coming up, Harry retorted, 'Well, I certainly think he's had a raw deal at your hands, yes.'

'And so you set me up. You must care about him a lot to let him persuade you to do that. Or was it your own idea?' he sneered.

'No, it was not. It wasn't anybody's idea. It just happened. And I'm sorry.'

'Not half as sorry as you would have been if your boyfriend had done what he wanted and marked my face. It could have held up the film for weeks. And you, lady, would have been out of a job.'

'He isn't my boyfriend.'

'What then—your lover?'

'No! I told you, he's a neighbour and a fellow actor. I met him in the pub and he told me he'd been offered the part of the police detective in the film. He was jubilant. He really thought he was getting somewhere at last.' Harry's voice hardened and she looked at Rex accusingly. 'But the next time I met him he said that you had intervened and insisted on giving the part to an actor of your choice. So he was out of work again and his wife has obviously had enough and has left him.'

'And you believed him?'

'I had no reason not to,' Harry retorted.

Rex gave a derisory laugh. 'No, I guess you hadn't at that. And is that why you gave me the cold shoulder at the party?'

Harry hesitated, then nodded. 'Yes.'

He gave her a shrewd look. 'But there were other reasons, weren't there?'

'Well—perhaps.'

'So what else have you got against me? I'd like to know—just in case I ever go into another pub with you,' he said sardonically.

Harry bit her lip, wondering whether or not to tell him of her prejudices, but decided that the angry mood he was in, Rex wasn't likely to listen with any degree of sympathy or understanding. And why should she, anyway? After all, it was he who had done the dirty on Mike in the first place. So her voice was cool as she said,

'I hardly think they would be of any interest to you. And now, if you don't mind, I'd like to go home.' She looked pointedly at where he was still holding her wrist.

'Well, I damn well do mind. Do you realise what that could have led to back there? Still could, in fact. It only needs one person in that pub to go to the Press and it could be all over the newspapers tomorrow that I was mixed up in a fight. And bad publicity like that wouldn't be good for me, my television series or this film. Had you thought of that?' Harry opened her mouth, but before she could speak he added disparagingly, 'No, don't tell me—that didn't occur to you, either. Lady, you're either a liar or real dumb.'

'I am not dumb! *And* I'm not a liar,' Harry snapped back. 'It was *you* who wanted to go to a pub, not me. Going out with you was the last thing I wanted.' She glared up at him, bright sparks of anger in her hazel eyes. 'And if you hadn't insisted on giving the part to one of your friends this would never have happened. There's nothing that makes me angrier than this kind of—of favouritism. Especially in show business, where there are so many good actors looking for jobs. It just isn't fair!'

Rex looked down into her angry face and slowly let go of her wrist to thrust his hands into his pockets. 'Yeah. But maybe you should have checked before you took Mike's word for it. It was one of the US backers who insisted on the switch, not me. Goodnight, Harry.'

He turned and began to walk away. Harry looked after him with a frown for a moment before she began to walk in the opposite direction. Then something occurred to her and she turned and ran after him. 'Rex, wait.'

He stood still and let her come up to him, looked down at her with a withdrawn expression on his handsome face. 'Well?'

'I meant to tell you before but—but arguing with you put it out of my head. I wanted to thank you for not hurting Mike. He'd obviously had a lot to drink and he was very unhappy—but you weren't to know that, of course. You could quite easily have knocked him down. I'm—I'm grateful that you didn't.'

Rex's jaw tightened for a moment, then he gave a shrug. 'Yeah, sure.' And he turned and strode away again, leaving Harry to hurry to join Emma in the car.

'You've been ages,' Emma complained as Harry got in. 'I'm freezing.'

'Sorry. We'll be home in a minute.'

Emma looked at her and burst out, 'I can find my own way home if you want to go to his flat with him.'

'*What* did you say?' Harriet demanded as she turned to look at the other girl.

'He fancies you! I know he does.'

'So what? Do you seriously think that I want to go back to his flat?'

'He would have asked you if I hadn't been there,' Emma said, half accusingly.

'So it was a good job you *were* there, then, wasn't it?' Harry said as she started the car. 'But I wouldn't even have gone out with him for a drink if you hadn't wanted to go. I didn't particularly want to.'

Emma looked at her curiously. 'Did he ask you to go to bed with him when you were alone with him just now?'

Harry smiled rather grimly. 'Quite the opposite. We had a row about Mike. Sex, thank goodness, was the last thing Rex had on his mind.'

'Don't you like him at all?'

Harriet shrugged. 'Oh, he's very attractive physically, I'll give him that. But boy, does he know it! He thinks he only has to smile at a woman and she'll throw herself at his feet.'

'Well, he certainly smiled at you often enough. He hardly took his eyes off you the whole time we were in the pub. He really fancies you, Harry.'

'I doubt it. He's probably just intrigued by the fact that I'm not drooling over him like everybody else, that's all.'

'I don't think he's like that,' Emma declared. 'I think he's nice—even though he preferred you to me.'

Harriet laughed. 'There you are, you see. The man has shocking taste for a start! Oh, come on. Let's forget him. I'm fed up with Rex Kynaston.' And she quickly drove the short distance to the house.

But when they'd got home and gone to bed, Harry lay awake for some time, thinking about Rex and the way he'd given her that special smile. The smile he probably reserved for girls he wanted to attract, she thought resentfully, and determined not to let him get under her defences again. Rex Kynaston, of all people! Why, he was the last man she would want to fall for. Not that he would be at all interested in her again, after that nasty little episode with Mike and her row with him afterwards.

And, anyway, Emma had been quite wrong. He had just wanted someone to while away a few hours with, that was all. So, what better than two attractive girls? Anyway, he would forget all about them once he met some well-known actresses or some society girls. And the film company would make sure he met some and was seen out with them, because it would all be good publicity for the film.

Satisfied with her cynical reasoning, Harriet snuggled into the pillow to go to sleep, but strangely her mind was filled by the picture of Rex so easily overpowering Mike and yet not taking any action in reprisal. With that, and the memory of his smile, she eventually fell into slumber.

Most films are shot out of sequence, the producers having to take advantage of the weather and the availability of the locations they want to use, so the scene that Harry was to shoot with Rex the next morning came a little later in the film, when he tried to get her alone at the flat to talk to her. Harry had to try and shut him out and he had to force his way in and question her about his dead fiancée.

Harry didn't see Rex until after she'd been to makeup and had put on her clothes for the part. The director called her over and Rex was standing beside him. As Harriet walked towards them she deliberately didn't look at Rex, although she was aware that his eyes were on her. She tried to feel very calm, very impersonal, but as she drew near her heart began to beat a little faster and her eyes were inexorably drawn to his. She had been right; he was watching her, his lips twisting into a small smile of cynical satisfaction when she finally had to acknowledge him.

'Morning, Harry,' the director greeted her. 'All ready to start shooting?' When she nodded, he added, 'Good. Why don't you and Rex go over to that empty part of the stage and give it a run through? I'll join you in a few minutes; I've just got to see the chief gaffer.'

They threaded their way round the back of the various sets to a comparatively empty and quiet place in the studio, away from the lights and the frenzied activity that always seemed to go with the making of a film. Harry was carrying her script and opened it at the scene they were to rehearse, although she didn't need to.

'It's on page twenty-three,' she said helpfully when she looked up and saw that Rex hadn't even opened his script.

'I know. Did you get home OK?'

'Yes, thanks. Did you?' she added reluctantly.

'Sure. I took a cab back to my apartment.'

His eyes ran over her, but his expression was withdrawn and Harry couldn't tell if he was still angry with her or not. Quickly she said, 'Shall we start? I'll pretend I'm on one side of the door.'

But Rex wasn't at all in a hurry to start work, and it seemed that he wasn't angry after all, because he said, 'I could still use a guide to show me round London.'

Harry's face tightened. 'I'm sure Emma would...'

'I'm not asking Emma, I'm asking *you*,' Rex cut in forcefully, his eyes darkening.

She looked at him for a moment, then said stiffly, 'You're supposed to ring the bell.'

Rex came to stand on the other side of their imaginary door and lifted his hand. 'OK, I'm ringing it.'

Harry went through the action of partly opening the door, seeing who it was and trying to slam it shut, but Rex barged his way in. He caught hold of her arm as she moved away, jerking her round to face him. But instead of saying his lines, he said, 'Will you come out with me for a drink tonight—just the two of us? Maybe we could pick up from where we'd got to before your actor friend—interrupted us.'

'I didn't realise that we'd got anywhere,' Harry answered as off-puttingly as she could.

Rex's voice grew softer, almost caressing. 'On the contrary, I was beginning to think we were reaching some kind of—understanding.'

He meant that smile they'd exchanged, of course, those few moments when they had been on the same wavelength. A sexual wavelength? Yes, perhaps it had been for Rex, but for Harry it had been more of an emotional rapport.

She hesitated and Rex said, 'And besides, you owe me for letting your friend break up our evening last night.'

Harry's head came up at that, and she remembered the last film she'd been in where the star had used sexual coercion. 'You're mistaken,' she said coldly. 'That was none of my doing, and I don't owe you a thing. Let's get on with the rehearsal, shall we?'

Rex frowned. 'Not until you agree.'

'Don't you ever bother to listen to what people say to you?' Harry demanded. 'I said no.'

'I don't remember those lines in the script.' The director's voice behind them made Rex step away from her, a frown of annoyance in his eyes, but whether from the interruption or because of her refusal, Harry wasn't sure. She quickly turned to greet the director, grateful for his timely arrival. He began to go through the scene with them, but for the first few minutes Harriet was unable to concentrate; she was too aware of Rex standing beside her and the tension he emanated.

When the director had finished, they walked it through and this time Rex spoke the correct lines, but it wasn't all acting when he raised his voice in anger or when his fingers tightened when he held her arm.

'Good! That's marvellous,' the director exclaimed at the end. 'Let's go over to the set and rehearse it again for lighting and sound.'

It was quite a long scene and it took all morning to shoot, first filming it from Rex's angle and then Harry's. As the morning progressed, Harry had to admit that Rex was a better actor than she'd expected and, even more important, he didn't try to hog the best camera shots for himself all the time. But if her feelings towards him had softened, she didn't let it show. The little undercurrent of tension was still there between them, and when they weren't acting together Harry moved away to sit and wait, or else chatted to Emma and Julie, who were watching. She was angry with herself for letting Rex have this effect on her, and tried hard to shake it off, but found herself avoiding his eyes, unable to look him directly in the face.

But on the set she *had* to look at him, and he took full advantage of the fact, his eyes asking their own questions as he played the scene. In the film she had to refuse to answer his questions and make him angry, and it wasn't difficult for him to show that emotion, it was quite near the surface, anyway. 'That was great,' the director enthused. 'You really rubbed sparks off each other. OK, everyone, we'll break for lunch now,' he declared after glancing at his watch.

Harry went to change, so was late getting to the studio cafeteria, but Emma had saved her a place at the table she was sharing with Julie and some of the girls from make-up and wardrobe. Glancing across the room, Harriet saw that Rex was sitting with the director and some of the other production staff, but he looked up as she came in, his eyes following her across the room.

That afternoon they were shooting a short scene of Rex with Emma and Julie, and then going on to a nearby location that had been chosen to show the road in which the flat was supposed to be situated. Here Rex was to wait for Harry to come home from work, so it had to be shot in the early evening when the light was right.

It had been a long day and Rex had been in every scene; he had a right to be tired, but he seemed as vital as ever as he joked with the make-up girl and went over to sign autographs for the small crowd that had gathered to watch. As they rehearsed the scene, Harriet was aware of him as much now as she had been this morning. Only this time he didn't have to touch her, so she couldn't feel the extra pressure of his hands or have her heart jump at his closeness. But, perhaps because they were at a distance and because she had to show antagonism, there was again that electric tension that brought the spark of realism to their acting.

When the director finally called it a wrap, Harriet gave a long sigh and closed her eyes for a moment as she relaxed. Going into the caravan that they used as a make-up room, she sat down and put her hands up to her neck muscles, only now aware of how deeply she had been concentrating.

'Tired?' the make-up girl asked sympathetically.

'No. Just tense. Lord, what I wouldn't give for a massage.'

The caravan rocked a little and someone came in as Harriet spoke, but before she could turn round to see who it was, Rex put his hands on her neck, gently moving hers out of the way. 'I'm pretty good at massage. Let's see if I can help.'

Harry immediately tried to move away but his strong hands held her down in her seat.

'Stay still,' he commanded. 'Just lean your head forward and close your eyes.'

There wasn't much else she could do except obey him; but at first she held herself stiffly, resenting his action. How dared he just walk in here and think he could handle her like this? Rex must have felt her rigidity, but his hands continued to stroke the muscles of her neck, firmly but gently. He's done this before a few times, Harry thought cynically, but even so she slowly began to relax, the skill in his hands gradually easing all the tensions away.

'Why won't you come out with me tonight?' Rex murmured when she was completely relaxed, her eyes closed, and beginning to enjoy it.

She tried to look round, startled that he should ask her such a question in front of the make-up girl. But Rex said, 'It's all right, she's gone.' His hands pushed her collar aside, came round and began to stroke her throat, slowly travelling up the long column to her chin. 'So?' he repeated. 'Why not? We could go some place and have dinner. We can talk, get to know one another.'

His hands were warm, caressing, and had already roused an ache of awareness in her, but Harriet suddenly broke free of his hold and stood up, turning round to face him, her eyes alight with anger. 'Has it occurred to you that I may not want to get to know you? You may think you're God's gift to women, Rex, but I don't . . '

Rex's dark eyes suddenly filled with anger and he reached out and caught her wrist, silencing her. 'Don't be damn silly,' he rasped out.

His grip tightened and he loomed over her, glaring down into her angry face. Tension rose like a giant wave, and for a moment Harry thought that he was going to kiss her. She gave a little gasp and stiffened to resist him, but then he dropped her wrist and turned away, thrusting his hands into his pockets. He strode the length of the caravan, cluttered with all the make-up and hair-dressing equipment, his shoulders hunched in anger. But when he reached the door he hesitated and turned to face her again.

'Look,' he said with sudden determination, 'some-where along the line this has gone all wrong. I admit I was intrigued when you gave me the cold shoulder, but when we were out last night I realised I really wanted to get to know you. But then that guy came along and—well, I really thought you'd set me up.'

He paused as if expecting Harriet to speak, but she'd denied it enough times already, she wasn't about to do so again.

'Last night it all seemed to point that way,' Rex said in explanation. He shrugged. 'But I guess I was wrong. I'm sorry.' His eyes went to her face, but Harry had lowered her head and he couldn't read her expression. 'So—don't you think that maybe now we could start over?'

Slowly she lifted her head to look at him down the length of the caravan. 'I don't owe you anything, Rex,' she told him directly.

He nodded. 'No, I guess not.' He started to walk towards her, looking so arrantly masculine and determined that Harry's heart jumped, her blood surging through her veins. 'So,' he said softly, reaching out for her. 'Will you come out with me tonight?'

Harry immediately put her hands behind her back, where he couldn't reach them. 'No,' she said and he frowned, but then added, 'Not—not tonight.'

Rex's brow cleared and he began to smile. 'When, then?'

'I—I don't know. I'd like to—think about it.'

'What is there to think about?' he demanded impatiently. 'You either want to come out with me or you don't.'

'It isn't that simple,' Harry disagreed.

'Why not? I don't understand.'

'No, I don't suppose you do. But—well, there are reasons.'

'You said that before. Tell me,' he commanded.

Harry gave a rather dry smile at his impervious tone, but shook her head. 'Not now. Perhaps—some other time.'

Although the words were hesitant, her tone was decisive and Rex realised he wasn't going to get any further with her by arguing. Perhaps he might have tried other methods of persuasion, but there was the sound of voices outside and someone—very tactfully—knocked on the door. He opened it at once and nodded to Harry. 'See you, then.' His eyes held hers for a moment, but she didn't reply and he turned and strode through the door.

None of the three girls was needed on the set the following day, and Harry, for one, was very glad of the reprieve. Only two days of working with Rex and already she felt overpowered by him. Having an unaccustomed lie-in, she tried to analyse her feelings about him, but found that she was hopelessly confused. She had started off by being antagonistic because of the rumours she'd heard about his payment for the film, and this had been enforced by the way he'd seemed to manipulate people when she'd first met him, but, loath as she was to admit it, she had to acknowledge that there was a certain charisma about him, quite apart from his physical good looks, that acted like a magnet. Was it the legendary star quality that everyone talked about? she wondered.

Well, whatever it was, she wasn't about to fall for it. Pushing the bedclothes aside, Harriet sat up. Rex's egotistical assumption that she would want to go out with him, despite what had happened, had angered her more than a little. She was a very attractive girl and was used to men running after *her*, not lifting their little finger and expecting her to come to heel like a pet dog. OK, so Emma and Julie as well as most of the other women in the unit were drooling over him, but Rex needn't think that she was going to do the same. Someone had to show a little feminine independence, for heaven's sake! But his apology yesterday had gone a long way towards softening her feelings towards him, and suddenly her thoughts were in turmoil again.

Putting on her track suit, Harry went jogging round the streets for half an hour, and arrived home to find a florist's van waiting outside the house, the driver standing by the van, chatting to one of her women neighbours. 'Here she is,' the neighbour announced when she jogged up to them. 'This is Miss Sutton.'

'Got some flowers for you, luv,' the driver said in a strong cockney accent. Opening the back door of the van, he put a big basket of red roses into her hands.

'And there's these as well.' And he brought out a beautiful bouquet of mixed flowers.

'Oh, aren't they lovely!' the neighbour exclaimed. 'Who are they from, Harry?' she asked nosily.

Harriet didn't really have to guess, but she dutifully opened the envelope and took out the card. It said simply, 'Forgive me? R.'

Taking the flowers indoors, Harry arranged them in vases and sat back in a chair, contemplating them while she drank a cup of coffee. Did Rex always send his girls flowers, she wondered, or just when he wanted to apologise for something? But somehow she couldn't see Rex apologising too often. Or even having to. Most women, she thought, would forgive him almost anything. And she knew in her heart that she, too, had forgiven him. Not that there was much to forgive, if she looked at it honestly. It had been an obvious assumption that she had taken him to the pub so that Mike could pick a fight with him, and Harry blamed herself for not having realised that Mike might be there.

But that was over now, and the flowers had served as a reminder—not that she needed one—that she must make up her mind whether to go out with Rex or not. Her instinct was to refuse and keep well away from him. Experience had taught her that big stars were bad news. And she had fully expected Rex to be the same, act the same. But there was something about him that excited and attracted her. Basic sex appeal? she wondered. Harry hoped it wasn't, hoped she had more sense and taste than to fall for only that. But there was certainly something about him that made her feel 'yes' when she ought to say 'no'.

When Emma came in from shopping, she found Harriet still sitting in the chair, surrounded by flowers. 'My God,' she exclaimed. 'Who's died?'

Harry laughed. 'No one—yet.'

'Who are they from?' Emma bent to smell one of the roses and turned to Harriet, her eyes wide. 'They're not from Rex?' And when Harry nodded, 'Wow! I *told* you he fancied you. He'll probably inundate you with presents until...' She stopped rather abruptly.

'Well, go on, why don't you finish it?' Harry said wryly. 'Until he gets what he wants. Namely, me.'

'Are you going to go—out with him?' Emma asked curiously.

'Why don't you say what you really mean?'

'All right, are you going to go to bed with him?'

'The one might not necessarily lead to the other,' Harry pointed out coolly.

'Are you kidding?' Emma said in disbelief. 'This is Rex Kynaston we're talking about. You know his reputation as well as I do.'

Harry looked at her unhappily. 'Yes, I suppose so.' She stood up restlessly.

'Are you even contemplating it?' Emma asked in astonishment. 'I thought you didn't even like him.'

'I'm not sure that I do. But he can be—very persuasive.' She turned in sudden anger. 'Why does it have to be one thing or the other? Surely it must be possible to just go out with him and get to know him first, like any other man?'

Emma looked at her and grinned. 'Something tells me that going out with Rex would be playing with fire. You either want to get burnt or you don't. And if you don't— well, that's a risk you'll just have to take, won't you?'

'But surely...' Harry broke off and looked at Emma's grinning face, picked up a cushion and threw it at her. 'Oh, to hell with Rex! Come on, let's go round the Chinese and get some dinner.'

They shot several short scenes in the studio the next morning, and in the afternoon moved to a local park where they were to shoot the three girls walking along together, discussing the murder and Rex's attempts to solve it. The sun was shining brightly and it was great to work outside for a change. As usual, it took the technicians quite a while to get everything ready for shooting. The three girls sat together while they waited, chatting desultorily, half-asleep in the heat. Rex wasn't in this scene at all, and they expected him to have gone back to his flat, but presently a car drew up and deposited him at the unit.

'Hi,' he greeted them, strolling over to sit beside them.

'You're a devil for punishment,' Emma told him. 'Why don't you take the afternoon off?'

He shrugged. 'I've no place to go.'

'You could have visited some of those places in London we told you about.'

He smiled at Emma, then looked past her to Harry, his eyes lingering on her face. 'Being a tourist is no fun on your own. I need a Londoner to take me round.'

He paused, obviously waiting for Harriet to answer him, and after a moment she said, 'That wouldn't be any good. Londoners never bother to do the tourist sights; they're too familiar with them. Any American tourist would probably know the place better in two weeks than someone who's lived here all their life.'

Emma looked from one to the other of them, then got to her feet saying, 'I'm thirsty. Let's go and get a drink, Julie.'

'What? Oh, yes. All right.' After catching a meaningful look from Emma, Julie got up too.

Harriet shot Emma a fulminating look, but the two of them walked off to the catering wagon, leaving Harry alone with Rex. She went to get to her feet to follow them, but Rex caught her wrist. 'No, stay and talk a minute. Please.'

Harry hesitated, words of refusal on her lips, but he *had* said 'please', and he was looking at her earnestly, without challenge or mockery in his expressive dark eyes. She nodded, 'All right,' and went to sit beside him again, but Rex stood up.

'Let's walk for a while,' he suggested.

They moved away from the unit, down a path and into the shade thrown by a row of old oak trees. Rex didn't speak at once; it was only when they'd got out of sight of the film crew that he stopped and turned to her. He was wearing a shirt, open almost down to his waist, and faded denim jeans stretched tight across his hips. Harriet felt a flutter of sexual awareness and quickly turned her head away, her throat suddenly dry.

Mistaking her action, Rex's face hardened. 'You know,' he burst out, 'I really thought that we might be able to just talk things out. Sensibly, and quietly. And that I might find out just what it is you've got against me. But you don't even want to listen to me. You're turning away from me before I can even begin to...'

Harry swung round to face him. 'I'm not—turning away from you,' she broke in forcefully, but then her voice trailed off as she looked into his eyes. 'I'm not,' she finished lamely.

Rex took a step forward and half lifted his hands to take hold of her, but then stopped. 'OK.' His eyes grew warm. 'OK, so let's talk.'

But he didn't seem to be in any hurry, so after a moment Harriet said, 'What—what did you want to say?'

His eyes left hers reluctantly. 'Well, I guess I was going to say that we seem to have started off all wrong. And I wanted to find out if there was anything I could do about that. If you tell me what reasons you have to— dislike me, disapprove of me—I don't even know which it is.' He looked at her hopefully for a moment but, when she didn't speak, went on, 'Look, Harry, a lot of things get written about movie stars and television stars that are either exaggerated out of proportion or maybe aren't even true at all. If you've read something about me that you don't like, won't you at least give me a chance to explain?'

He spoke earnestly, and Harry was inclined to believe him. She moved a couple of paces away and reached up to pick a leaf from the tree, looking at its formation with absorbed interest, thinking about his reputation with women. 'I did hear something about you,' she admitted slowly.

'What was it? Tell me.'

'No.' She shook her head. 'It made me angry because it corroborated something that I was already angry about. It made you a part of it, you see.'

'Aren't you going to tell me what it is? I'd really like to know.'

'Maybe one day. Now is hardly the time or place.'

He moved a little nearer, his eyes on her bent head. 'Does that "one day" mean that you've forgiven me?' he asked softly.

A woman walking a dog came towards them along the path and Harriet moved to get out of her way. Rex did the same thing, which brought them very close, almost touching.

'Does it?' he asked urgently as soon as the woman had passed.

'Well, I suppose we could start again,' Harriet temporised. 'Without any—major bias.'

Rex laughed, sure of himself again. 'And is that as far as you're prepared to relent? I'm beginning to think you're a hard-hearted woman, Harry.'

She smiled and looked down at the leaf in her hand again. 'I've never been out with an American actor before. Or any kind of American, if it comes to that.'

'We're no different to anyone else.'

'Oh, but I think you are.'

His face became serious again. 'Tell me how I'm different.' He leant against the trunk of the gnarled old tree, waiting, aware that a lot would depend on his reaction to what she said now.

'You go too fast for me. Oh, I'm not saying that some English men aren't as fast, or even faster if it comes to that. But they don't have, perhaps, your experience— your ability to manipulate women,' she finished slowly.

Rex let out his breath in a whistle. 'Phew! That's a tough one. Is that really how I seem to you?' He paused for a moment, then came over and put a casual arm across her shoulders and began to walk slowly along again.

Harry was tall, but Rex was quite a bit taller than she, and it felt good to walk like that, in close companionship. But she didn't let him see that she felt that way. She was still far from sure of her feelings towards him, and even less sure of how Rex felt towards her. They had known each other for such a short time. Harriet got the rather overwhelming sensation of being poised at the top of a helter-skelter ride, and if she wasn't careful she would go hurtling down the slide at breakneck speed at any moment. In some ways it was an exhilarating experience, but most of the time she felt just plain scared.

Referring to her last remark, Rex said musingly, 'I guess I do have some experience at handling women. It's something I've had to learn, like it or not.' He gave a short laugh. 'It's a case of self-preservation most of the time. When you get a role in a television programme like mine, playing opposite a new leading lady every week, and having to appear as a playboy type who can pull any woman he wants . . .' He shrugged. 'Well, I guess the image kind of rubs off and you get these girls who all want to—er—meet you. Most of them are hoping to get a part in the television show, of course,' he added, his face and voice becoming very grim for a moment. 'But I suppose I've just learnt how to make them back off—most of the time.'

Harry lifted her head to look at him and said, her voice dripping with sympathy, 'Why, Rex, you poor thing. I had no idea. It must be a really hard life fighting off all those beautiful girls all the time. How you must hate it!'

He raised an eyebrow, fully aware that he was being teased. 'You wait till this film makes you into a star and you have men falling over themselves just to have their picture taken with you.' Coming to a halt, he kept his arm on her shoulders but turned her to face him. 'Although I'm beginning to suspect,' he added, 'that you're probably pretty good at keeping men at arm's length yourself.' His voice changed, lost its teasing note. 'You're a beautiful girl, Harry. You must have had plenty of experience of guys chasing you. Especially being an actress.'

There was a questioning note in his voice but she chose not to answer it, instead saying, 'What makes you so sure this film is going to be a hit?'

'I have a gut feeling about it. And the adrenalin's working right, isn't it?'

Harriet smiled, knowing what he meant. 'Yes,' she agreed. 'I rather think it is.'

'Good.' He put his other arm on her shoulders so that his head was close to hers. 'And will you make it a date tonight?'

'For dinner in a country pub?'

'For anything you want, Harry. Any place you want to go.'

She lifted her chin to regard him with cool hazel eyes. Harry was by no means naïve and was fully aware of what getting involved with Rex might lead to. She recognised, too, the subtle note in his voice that could be the prelude to a pass if she gave him the slightest encouragement or hint that that was what she wanted. So she said firmly, 'Dinner. And that's all. OK?'

His mouth twisted a little ruefully, but he nodded. 'OK, it's a bargain.' She went to turn away, but he held her still and said with suggestive challenge, 'In America, we always seal bargains with a kiss.'

But Harriet refused to be drawn. 'Really? In England, we just shake hands.'

'You're a tyrant, Harry,' Rex grumbled. 'Aren't you going to let me kiss you?'

'Certainly not. And besides, you've already managed to kiss me once.'

'Mmm,' he agreed with a grin. 'So you remembered, huh?'

'I generally do make a note of when a man kisses me against my will,' Harry informed him wryly.

He laughed. 'You have a really dry wit, you know that?' His eyes rested caressingly on her face. 'I can't wait to find out what it's like to kiss you when you're willing.'

His tone was so suggestive that to Harriet's annoyance she felt herself start to blush, but was saved from such an embarrassing fate when one of the runners in the crew came round the bend in the path and called out to her that they were ready to shoot.

'Tonight, then,' Rex said as they began to walk back. 'Tell me where you live and I'll pick you up in the limo.'

But Harry didn't take to that idea at all. 'You don't really want the film-company driver along, do you? Actually, your flat isn't that far from where I live, so why don't I pick you up?'

Rex hesitated only fractionally. 'OK. What time?'

'About eight?'

'OK, fine.' He looked at her. 'You English girls certainly do like to be independent, don't you?'

'It's a habit we've fought for,' Harriet laughed as she ducked out of his hold and began to run ahead. 'Call it our war of independence. You should know all about that,' she called. ''Bye.' And she ran on out of his sight.

As she reached the film crew Harry paused to still her beating heart, wondering why she felt so breathless, and then realised that she had launched herself from the top of the helter-skelter and was about to plunge down the dizzy spiral to heaven knew where.

CHAPTER FOUR

HARRY became involved in her part after that, and hardly noticed that Rex watched for a while and then left. When shooting was over, Harriet and Emma drove back to London together as usual, Harriet cutting skilfully through the traffic to get them there as quickly as possible.

'You seem to be in a hurry,' Emma commented as Harry took advantage of a gap to pull into the faster lane.

'I have a date tonight. I'm supposed to be meeting him at eight.'

'You didn't mention it this morning. Or hadn't you made it then? It couldn't be anything to do with that chat you had with Rex this afternoon, could it?' And when Harriet nodded rather sheepishly, Emma laughed and said, 'I knew you wouldn't be able to resist him for very long. Admit it, Harry, you're just like the rest of us. You think he's gorgeous, too.'

'There is something about him,' Harry agreed with a sigh. 'But I almost wish there wasn't.'

'But what a crazy thing to say. You're bound to have a wonderful time with him. And if his reputation is anything to go by—well, he's supposed to be as great a lover off-screen as he is on.'

'Look, I'm only going out for a meal with him. Nothing else,' Harriet said snappily. 'Just because I said I'd go out with him doesn't mean that I'm going to go to bed with him. Oh, hell! I knew how it would be. If anyone takes a photograph of us when we're out together it will be all over the papers that I'm just the latest addition to his long list of women. And I'm not like that, Emma. I'm not just a push-over.'

'Well, go somewhere where no one will take your picture,' Emma said practically. 'Then you won't have any problems. Although, quite frankly, I don't see what you're worried about. *I* wouldn't mind in the least having my name coupled with Rex's. It would be great publicity.'

'But hardly worth the price. Darn, I almost wish I hadn't said that I'd go out with him now.'

'But only almost,' Emma said teasingly.

Harry began to smile and then laughed. 'You're right. But it had better be worth it.'

It was in this kind of prickly, half-resentful mood that she went round to Rex's flat an hour or so later. There had been just enough time to have a bath, wash her hair and change into a rather stunning coral-coloured outfit of top and trousers that she hadn't worn before. It was in a silky material that looked loose and casual, but which clung in all the right places. It felt good and her mirror told her that it looked good too, the colour ideal for her dark hair and summer tan.

Rex's flat was in a block of luxury, short-lease service apartments, with a porter on duty at the desk in the foyer. Rex wasn't waiting for her, so Harry had to ask the porter to put a call through to him, but he came down straight away, dressed in dark blue trousers, a paler blue casual jacket and a silk shirt, open at the neck. He looked quite something, making Harriet's breath catch in her throat again, and from the appreciative way he looked her over, he obviously felt the same about her.

'Hi.' He came straight up to her and put his arm around her waist, much to the interest of the porter. 'You look beautiful.'

'Thanks. Let's go, shall we?' Harriet suggested quickly, acutely aware of eyes watching them.

Her car was just outside and Harriet went round to the driver's side, leaving Rex to get in the passenger seat. But after he'd bent to open the door, he said, 'Harry, I think we have a problem.'

'What problem?' she asked, impatient to get away from the watching porter.

'I don't think I'm going to fit into your car.'

'But you must be able to...' Harry looked at his big frame, and the smallness of her sports car. 'Oh dear, I see what you mean. Give it a try.'

'OK.' He tried a couple of times, but only by pushing the seat right back and sitting with his head more or less between his knees could he manage to get in and shut the door. By this time Harry was shaking with suppressed laughter, and he gave her a dark look. 'Next time we take the limo, OK?'

'But, Rex, this is so cosy.' And, unable to contain it any longer, she burst out laughing.

Reaching out a hand, Rex put it under her chin and turned her to face him. 'Do you realise this is ruining my image?'

Her eyes dancing, Harriet retorted, 'Good. I'm glad.' All her resentment had gone now, driven away by the absurdity of the incident.

Rex's eyebrows rose. 'Why? Because you want to take me down a peg or two?'

'No. Because it's you I want to go out with, not your image.'

For an instant his fingers tightened on her chin. 'Thanks,' he said sincerely. 'That means a hell of a lot.'

Leaning forward, he kissed her, lingeringly, on her mouth, his lips exploring hers gently, as if he'd never kissed a girl before. It was quite a kiss, and Harry would have liked it to go on much longer, but she didn't want to be kissed like that here, in such a well-lit place, so after only a short while she drew away. 'People can see us.'

'What? Oh, yeah, I guess so.' Rex didn't look as if he cared very much, but he drew back and let her start the car.

His shoulders took up most of the room, but Harriet was able to weave her way through the busy evening traffic with all the skill of a London taxi driver and, as her engine was far more powerful, with far greater speed.

'Who taught you to drive?' Rex asked after a few rather tense minutes.

Harry laughed. 'My father. He used to be quite a well known rally driver. I'm not going too fast for you, am I?'

'No, I'm used to speed. Don't you ever watch any of those car chases in my television series? It's just being so low on the ground and driving on the wrong side of the road that takes some getting used to.'

Reaching the motorway, Harriet put her foot down, and within twenty minutes they were pulling up outside a very old thatched-roof pub in a small country village. Rex extricated himself from the Lotus with some difficulty, and they went through into the low-ceilinged bar where he had to be careful to duck his head under the age-blackened beams. Almost everyone in the bar paused in their conversation to look them over. Harriet was used

to being looked at, because she was a beautiful girl, but
she wasn't used to being with someone so famous that
he was immediately recognisable, and she was very sensitive about it, disliking the loss of privacy. 'Shall we go
straight into the dining-room?' she suggested.

'No, we're going to have one of your famous warm
beers in here first,' Rex said firmly. 'Don't take any
notice. They'll soon get used to us.'

'You're very astute. I didn't realise my nerves were
showing. But you make it sound as if we're beings from
another planet.'

'Perhaps we are, out here. If we'd gone to a nightclub
or some classy place in London, we probably wouldn't
have been noticed.'

Harriet very much doubted that; Rex wasn't the kind
of man you could overlook. 'Do you usually go to that
kind of place?'

'Most times, I guess.' He ordered their drinks and they
sat on stools at the end of the bar where there weren't
any other people. 'Most of the girls I go out with expect
to be taken to classy places.'

'I see. So what does that make you think of me?' It
was an impulsive question, and Harry immediately
wished she hadn't asked it. Rex was just tonight's date,
nothing more; what did she care what he thought of her?
But she knew immediately that it did matter—very much.

Leaning an elbow on the bar, Rex looked at her and
said, 'I like it here—and I like you. I think you're very
English and very different to any other girl I've known.
And I'm quite sure that I want to get to know you much
better. Very much better.' And his hand covered hers as
he looked at her intently, his eyes sending their own
message.

Harriet's heart did a crazy kind of leap and she gave a shaky laugh. 'I bet you say that to all the girls,' she managed to say flippantly.

Rex grinned. 'Now who's being cute?'

And she thanked heaven that she hadn't taken him seriously. She asked him then about his career in America, a subject that carried them through into the dining-room and half-way through their meal, as Rex told her how he'd got started in television, about his house in Los Angeles and his penthouse apartment in New York.

'How terribly exciting,' Harriet remarked with false admiration in her voice. 'And to think that you were only working as a lifeguard when you were—er—discovered. Or isn't that true?'

Catching the derisive note, Rex raised a sardonic eyebrow and said, 'Sure, it's true. But I'd been through drama school, repertory and bit parts, the same as anyone else. I took the job as a beachguard because I needed to live between parts. If I'd got the lead in the series a few months earlier, they would have said that I was discovered working in a Chinese laundry!' Pausing to refill their wine glasses, he said, 'How about you? How did you get into show business?'

'Oh, I just got bitten by the bug doing school plays, and went on to drama school. I did a year in rep, then managed to get a few parts on the stage and on television and in one film. I've just been working my way up ever since.'

'And is this film your biggest part?'

Harriet nodded. 'Yes. I had to audition three times before I finally got it.'

'So it's important to you?'

'Yes, of course. If I make a success of this...' She shrugged. 'Well, it could lead to some really worthwhile parts. I might be able to choose what I want to do instead of having to take anything that's offered.'

'Was that from financial necessity?' Rex asked.

It was a very personal question and Harry didn't like it. 'Partly,' she answered stiffly. 'But the more work you do, the more often your face is seen and you're likely to be remembered by some casting director.'

'Maybe I'll be able to help you get some parts,' Rex offered. 'Have you ever considered working in America? Maybe I could get you a part in my series.'

He looked at her keenly as he said it, and Harry had the strange feeling that he was putting her through some kind of test.

Tilting her head to look at him, Harriet said coolly, 'Do you say that to all the girls, too?'

Rex's mouth twisted rather wryly. 'You don't give a guy a chance, do you? No, as a matter of fact I don't say that to all the girls.'

'Because you don't need to?' she suggested shortly.

'Because I don't *want* to. But you can act, you're lovely to look at, and I think the American viewers would go over big for your English accent and your cool English manner.'

He said the last three words rather sardonically, making Harriet look quickly at his face. 'Thank you,' she said rather stiltedly. 'But I'm not very likely to go to America.'

'Why not? I could show you around. You might even get to like it there.'

Shaking her head, Harry said, 'I'm hoping to get an audition to become a member of the Royal Shakespeare

Company at Stratford-upon-Avon when this film is finished.'

'Going in for the heavy stuff, huh?'

'It's what every British actor wants to do—appear at Stratford in Shakespeare.'

Strangely, Rex didn't seem at all disappointed. His voice was even light as he said, 'Well, I guess that even the offer of a part in America wouldn't tempt you away from that.'

'No.' Harriet said the word quite definitely, but she couldn't help wondering what her future might have been if she'd said yes. Somehow she couldn't imagine Rex having purely altruistic motives, and she rather cynically guessed that his offer entailed more than just a job. She looked at him across her glass. The meal was over and Rex was sitting back in his chair, completely relaxed, completely self-assured. Basically he had a hard face, she decided, with a strong profile and square jaw, but his features were softened by thick dark hair that fell forward on to his forehead, and by that crazy moustache. Harriet wasn't sure whether she liked the moustache or not. In plays, she had been kissed by men wearing false beards and whiskers, but stage kisses hardly counted; Rex was the first man with a moustache to kiss her for real.

He had been looking round the pub, interestedly examining a collection of old horse brasses that adorned the blackened beams, but he must have felt her eyes on him because he turned his head quickly and caught her watching him. His hand reached out to cover hers and he gave an experienced, knowing smile. It came to Harriet then, that most girls would have jumped at the chance of being shown round America by him—even without the offer of a job. To have an affair with Rex Kynaston must be quite an experience—until he let you know that it was over and he was ready to move on to the next girl! Did he let you down lightly and tactfully, Harry wondered, so that you remained friends and could look back on it as a happy time, or did he just throw you out like an old and broken toy?

'Ready to go?' Rex asked, his hand lightly stroking hers.

Harriet nodded and waited while he paid the bill—and signed a menu for the barmaid, who gazed up at him in awestruck admiration.

It was dark outside, but it was a warm, moonlit night and there were quite a few people sitting outside the pub at wooden tables having a drink, and there were even children still playing on the village green opposite.

'Let's take a walk, shall we?' Rex suggested. 'I don't think I'm quite ready to fold myself into that car of yours yet.'

So they skirted the village green and turned into a lane that went past a row of cottages and then gave on to open fields, newly cut and harvested, the sweet smell of cut hay still hovering in the air. Rex had his arm across her shoulders as they walked, a habit he seemed to have, and they strolled slowly along in companionable silence, content to just savour the beauty and stillness of the night after their meal and the wine.

But presently they came to a footpath sign with a stile under it, leading to a path through a wood.

'Let's see where it goes to,' Rex said and stepped quickly over the stile, then leaned over it to offer his hand. 'Come on.'

But Harry hung back. 'It's dark in there. We won't be able to see where we're going.'

'Sure we will. We'll just go a short way.' Catching hold of her arm, he pulled her towards him.

'Rex, I don't...' But then Harriet heard a car coming along the lane and quickly climbed over the stile, realising how ridiculous it would look with Rex on one side and her on the other, engaged in a kind of tug-of-war.

It wasn't so dark in the wood, after all. The path was quite wide and the moon shafted down through the trees turning the night to silver. 'It reminds me of *A Midsummer Night's Dream*,' Harry murmured as she looked up at the moon. 'You expect Titania or Oberon to appear from behind every tree.'

'Mm,' Rex agreed. 'The kind of night when you ought to be able to make a wish and have it come true.' He stopped and turned her round to face him. 'Make a wish,' he commanded.

'All right.' Harriet closed her eyes and pretended to concentrate, but she didn't make a wish; her thoughts were too chaotic. Her pulses had begun to race and she had that heady feeling as if she was drunk, although she'd been careful not to have too much wine. She was very aware of Rex's hands on her arms, of his closeness and the faint, tangy, clean smell of his aftershave.

'OK,' Rex said softly. 'Tell me what you wished.'

Swallowing to clear her dry throat, Harriet shook her head. 'I can't do that. If you tell it won't come true. Now it's your turn.'

Rex gave her one of his lazy smiles. 'OK, I'm wishing.' But he didn't close his eyes, keeping them on her face instead. His hands tightened and he drew her slowly towards him until her body was close against his. 'Make my wish come true, Harry,' he said softly, then took her lips in a kiss of deepening passion. His hands moved down her body, holding her hips close against his as he arched her against him. He kissed her hungrily, almost as if he hadn't had a woman in a long time, forcing her mouth to open under his, to let his probing tongue explore the moistness within.

Harriet gave a little gasp and pulled away, but Rex immediately put his hand in her hair, holding her still so that he could go on kissing her. The rising hardness of his body pressing against her worked a magic of its own, filling her with an aching desire that made her put her arms round his neck and return his kiss with a sudden fierce surge of longing. Rex's arms tightened round her and he said, 'Oh, God, honey,' on a thick note of passion.

Then there was no time for words as they embraced ardently, each on fire with a desperate, urgent yearning to be held and touched and loved. Rex's mouth left hers as he kissed her neck and throat, his breath hot and unsteady. He parted the cross-over front of her blouse and went on down, kissing the shadowed valley between her breasts, his moustache soft and silky against her skin. His hands fumbled with her blouse, trying to undo it.

'How the hell do you get this thing off?' he muttered.

Her head in a whirl, Harriet gropingly tried to regain her senses and step away from him. 'You—you don't. I...'

But Rex pulled her roughly back and kissed her greedily. 'You're driving me crazy, honey,' he said urgently. 'I want you so much. Let's go back to my flat. Let's go to bed.'

Harriet took a deep breath and shook herself free of his embrace, literally holding him at arm's length. 'Look,' she said unevenly. 'You promised that we would just go out to dinner tonight. That was all.'

'But, darling, it's different now. You want to go to bed too now, don't you? Don't you?' he repeated, brushing her arm aside and drawing her to him.

But to have her emotions so crudely described filled Harry with angry embarrassment, and she quickly pushed him away. 'No, I damn well don't!' And she turned and began to hurry back down the path.

'Wait!' Rex started to come after her, but a cotton-wool cloud, its edges tipped with iridescent silver, drifted across the sky, plunging the wood into sudden darkness as if someone had turned off the moon.

Harriet knew that she ought to stand still and wait until she could see again, but she plunged on in what she thought was the direction of the road. Some leaves brushed against her face, scaring her for a minute, but she pushed them aside and went on. Behind her she heard Rex call her name and then curse the darkness. 'Harry, wait!' Her sleeve caught on something and she turned to free it, but just as she did so there was a sudden noise in the undergrowth and a bird flew out right in front of her face. Starting with fright, Harriet shrieked and tore her sleeve free, then turned to run back the way she'd come, but she had only taken a few paces when Rex reached her. Harriet grabbed his jacket, more than grateful for his size and strength.

'Harry, what is it? Why did you scream?'

'Something jumped out and frightened me.'

'You poor darling.' Rex's arms went round her protectively. 'Did you see what it was?'

The moon came out again and she realised that she was clinging to him. 'It was a bird. I'm sorry,' she added stiffly, 'I don't usually scare that easily.'

Letting go of him, she tried to move away, but Rex held her still. 'Why did you run off like that?' he demanded. 'It was a crazy thing to do.'

'Maybe I felt a little crazy. Can we get out of this wood before the moon goes in again? We don't want to get lost.'

'All right.' But when they looked round there was no sign of the path. For a terrible minute Harriet thought they really were lost, but Rex looked up at the moon, took her hand firmly in his and said, 'This way.'

They had to skirt some clumps of brambles, and Rex helped her to jump a stream, but he led her unerringly back to the road, although further down from the path on which they'd gone in. Harriet stopped to pull a leaf from her hair. 'How did you find your way so easily? I was completely lost.'

'I was a boy scout.' Putting his hands on his hips, Rex stood and looked at her. 'Just what is it with you, Harry? You surely knew that after a clinch like that I'd ask you to go to bed with me. So why make all this fuss, as if I was attacking your virtue or something?'

His voice was dry, sarcastic, implying that any virtue she might have had was long since gone.

'I hardly know you,' Harry began to protest. 'I don't . . .'

'What is there more to know?' Rex broke in. 'What the hell do you want—a reference?'

'Oh God! You're so damn *clinical*!' Turning angrily away, Harry began to walk back towards the pub.

Rex caught up with her in two strides and turned her round to face him. 'Just what do you want from me, then?' he demanded angrily.

'Nothing! I don't want anything from you.'

'Oh, yes you do.' Taking hold of her wrists, Rex gazed down at her, his face set. 'You want to have sex just as much as I do. The way you kissed me back there proves that. So why this act of playing hard to get?'

'Hard to get? My God, I've only known you a week!'

'So what difference does that make?'

'It makes all the difference in the world to me. Look,' her voice trembling, Harriet tried to explain, 'strange as it may seem to you, I don't go to bed with men—men I've just met. And I'm not going to go to bed with you just because you happen to be America's number five sex symbol, and because I want to—to try you out. For heaven's sake, Rex, what does that make either of us? I don't want sex just for sex's sake. And anyway, in my book it's called making love and there has to be some—some emotion involved.'

Rex's face had hardened as she spoke. He waited until she'd finished, then said derisively, 'So you want it all dressed up as romance. And are you already in love with me, Harry?'

She gave him a startled look. 'In love with you? No, of course not.'

'So just what emotion was it that made you kiss me the way you did back there?' he demanded with a definite sneer in his tone.

Harriet blinked, then gave a small, puzzled shake of her head. 'I—I don't know. I suppose because you know how to kiss too well.'

'Well, thanks for that. But I did arouse emotion in you, Harry. It's called good old-fashioned lust. And that's all two people need to go to bed together. They don't need any of this "hearts and flowers" stuff. You don't need love to enjoy each other's bodies, to give each other pleasure.'

She stared up at him, seeing his face hard and set in the moonlight, which seemed a harsh light now. 'Do you really believe that? Or is it some kind of guard that you've put up to protect yourself? Don't you feel anything for the women you go to bed with?'

'Sure, I feel something. I feel grateful. And happy,' he added with a crooked grin.

'Then I feel sorry for you,' Harriet said shortly. 'Oh, let's go back to the car. I'm getting cold.'

'OK. Do you want my jacket?'

'No.' She shook her head and strode quickly back through the village, silent and empty now that the pub had closed. She walked straight and tall, her head held high, but wishing heartily that she'd never agreed to go out with him tonight.

Reaching the car, she got in and waited while Rex wedged himself inside. 'Have you ever thought of getting a regular-sized car?' he asked.

'Lotuses are the best cars there are, and this one does me fine,' she retorted.

She reached out to turn on the ignition, but Rex put his hand over hers to stop her. 'Why are you so angry with me, Harry?'

'I'm not angry.'

'Yes, you are. You're angry because you're frustrated, but won't admit it. You want to go to bed with me and you will—some time soon. But I'm not going to make it easy for you by pretending that I'm in love with you. I keep all my acting for in front of the cameras. Life is for real.'

'I'm *not* going to let you make love to me.'

'Oh, but you are.' Reaching out a hand he gently stroked her face, but she jerked her head away. Rex laughed softly. 'You're going to go to bed with me, Harry—and on my terms, not on yours.'

Pushing aside his hand, Harriet started the car and accelerated out of the car park. She drove fast, but knew better than to let her emotions affect her driving. She was angry, she realised, but mostly with herself for having fallen for Rex, the same as everyone else. And she had been crazy to think that she could go out with him and not have him proposition her, even though he'd promised he wouldn't.

The London streets were clear now, and she drove quickly to Rex's block, pulling up sharply in the covered portico outside. 'Goodnight, Rex,' she said shortly.

'Sure you don't want to come in and go to bed?' Harry merely glared at him and he laughed. 'You will, you know, sooner or later. And think of all the time we're wasting while you're playing games.'

'Will you please get out of my car?' Harriet bit out fiercely, the hold on her temper near to breaking point.

Rex laughed again, but opened the door and began to heave himself out. 'Goodnight, Harry. See you tomorrow.'

Thrusting her foot down on the accelerator pedal, Harriet shot away, making him leap back out of the way. The house was only a short distance from the flat and she was still seething with anger when she reached it.

'Hi, Harry, how did it go?' Bob asked, looking up from the television set.

'Harry? Are you back already?' Emma bounced out of the kitchen, agog with curiosity. 'We didn't expect you back so soon.'

'Oh, didn't you?' Harriet answered crossly. 'I suppose you're like everyone else, and think that Rex Kynaston is so damn irresistible that I'd spend the night with him! Well, for your information, he just isn't my type!' And she ran upstairs, leaving them looking after her in astonishment.

Having to go to the film studios and face Rex the next morning was something Harriet could have done without, but the call sheet listed her for several scenes that day, and there was no way she could avoid it.

'You look as if you've had a heavy night,' the make-up girl remarked as she looked objectively at Harriet's face. 'I'll have to put extra make-up round your eyes.'

'I didn't sleep very well,' Harry explained.

The girl laughed. 'Nor would I, if I'd spent the night with Rex.'

Harry's eyes widened. 'I did not spend the night with him,' she exclaimed angrily.

'No? Oh, sorry, I didn't realise it was supposed to be a secret.'

Harry opened her mouth to deny it further, but then shut it again, knowing that it would be useless. Once a rumour like that got around a film unit, no amount of denials would put it out of people's minds. She wondered how on earth everyone had got to know that she had gone out with Rex, and so quickly. She certainly hadn't told anyone; so did that mean that Rex was boasting of his conquest of her, even though it was a lie? Her lips curled scornfully and she was fiercely glad that she'd turned him down. She, at least, knew the truth, even if no one else would ever believe it.

When she walked on to the set with Julie and Emma, Rex was already there, standing patiently in position while the technicians worked round him, getting the light and camera angles right. He looked across the set at her, waiting for her to speak to him, his eyes holding hers. But Harriet's chin came up defiantly and she merely returned his gaze in a silent battle of wills.

'Rex, if you could look this way, please,' the lighting cameraman asked, and he had to turn away.

They all three had a scene in which they appeared with Rex and the actor playing the police detective in the case. It was quite a long scene and rather a difficult one, with quite a lot of heated argument going on, and it was also to be interrupted by a phone call. They had to rehearse it several times before the director was satisfied, and even then it took them all morning and several takes before it was filmed exactly as he wanted it. Luckily, Rex didn't have to touch her in the scene, but there had to be tension between them in the way they looked at each other, an emotion Harriet didn't have to fake at all. She was acutely aware of what everyone on the set must think, and she took good care to keep well away from Rex in between takes. His lips curled in sardonic amusement when he watched her walk away, but he made no attempt to seek her out, apparently content to let the rumour he'd started work for him.

At one they broke for lunch, and Emma was free to go, as she wasn't needed in the afternoon. It was Friday, so she had decided to go home to Birmingham for the weekend.

'I'll drive you to the station, if you like,' Harriet offered.

'No, that's OK, you stay and finish your lunch. As a matter of fact, Rex has offered me a ride in his limo,' Emma answered.

'Well, he certainly doesn't waste any time,' Harry exclaimed. 'How can you let him use you like this?'

'He's giving me a lift, that's all.'

Harry gave her an old-fashioned look and Emma said sharply, 'Look, you didn't like it when people didn't believe that you hadn't been to bed with him, but now *you* don't believe that he's only giving me a lift. Which is hardly consistent, is it?'

'You're right,' Harry admitted. 'I'm sorry. Goodbye, Emma, have a good weekend.' But she couldn't help feeling extremely cynical as she watched Emma get into the big car with Rex beside her.

He was back promptly after lunch, though, to act in a scene that was mostly with Julie, Harry only coming into it at the end, in time to stop him getting any information out of the other girl. They rehearsed the scene and went through it again for the technicians, then had to sit around and wait for an adjustment to be made to the set before they could actually shoot. Julie went off to make a phone call and Rex strolled over to where Harriet was sitting talking to the continuity girl who, traitorously in Harriet's opinion, got up and went away, leaving Rex to sit in her vacant chair.

Harry's hand was leaning on the arm of her chair and Rex immediately took a firm grip on her wrist to stop her from getting up and walking away, as she tried to do.

'Emma said to say goodbye to you,' he told her, and when Harry didn't respond, added, 'She's a cute kid. Maybe she'd enjoy a night out on the town with me.'

'I'm sure she would,' Harry answered calmly.

Rex raised an eyebrow. 'You wouldn't be jealous?'

'Certainly not,' she flashed back, adding maliciously, 'I'm merely pleased to see you turning your somewhat dubious talents in a direction in which they might possibly be appreciated.'

'Ouch!' Rex winced, but looked at her admiringly. 'You're real sharp, Harry. I like that. Where would you like to go tonight?'

'With you? Nowhere.'

In no way put out, he said equably, 'OK, I'll choose. I'll pick you up at eight-thirty.'

'I do *not* want to go out with you.' Her voice rising, Harriet glared at him. 'And will you please let go of my hand?'

He shook his head at her. 'If you start shouting at me, Harry, everyone will think we're having a lovers' quarrel.'

'And just whose fault is it that they all think we're lovers in the first place?' she shot back at him. '*I* certainly didn't tell anyone that I was going out with you. A decision, by the way, that I infinitely regret. And I certainly wouldn't degrade myself by letting anyone think that I was just another name to add to your little black book!' she finished acidly.

Rex was looking at her in open appreciation. 'You know that saying about a woman being beautiful when she's angry?' he asked. 'Well, I'm really beginning to think you're the most beautiful woman I've ever known!'

Which was the most double-edged compliment Harriet had ever received. 'Oh, for heaven's sake!' she said angrily. 'Will you please listen to me?'

'I am listening. And you're way out of date; we playboys keep all the details of our women on computers, nowadays.'

Furious at his levity, Harry tried to jerk her hand free and get up, but Rex stopped her when she was only halfway out of her seat. His eyes grew serious. 'I'm sorry, Harry. I guess it's my fault. I told my driver I wouldn't need him last night because you were picking me up. That's all. The rumour must have started from him.'

'And I've just got to live with it, I suppose,' she said bitterly.

He grinned, his eyes mocking. 'Well, you could always live with me instead,' he retorted audaciously.

With an outraged exclamation, Harriet pulled her hand free and stalked to her dressing-room to wait until she was called for the take. She wondered if Rex really would turn up on her doorstep that evening, even though she'd turned him down so firmly. She wouldn't put it past him; he seemed to be capable of anything to get what he wanted. An attribute Harriet wasn't quite sure whether she disliked or admired. Getting out an emery board, she began to do her nails, but her thoughts drifted back to Rex, remembering how he'd taken Emma to the station and whether he really thought that something like that could make her jealous. She hadn't been in the least jealous of course, she told herself firmly. But then, in sudden honesty, realised just what this ache in her heart was and knew that she couldn't lie to herself any longer.

CHAPTER FIVE

THEY didn't finish filming until gone six that evening and it was a battle to get home against the traffic. Bob and Eric, the other two tenants, were at home, neither of them having a date that evening. Harry remembered Rex's half-threat to call for her at eight-thirty, but decided that he hadn't been serious and changed into casual jeans and a T-shirt. It was Eric's turn to make dinner and he was a good cook, having been brought up by a mother who believed in equality of the sexes. But it was Harry's turn to wash up afterwards and she was in the kitchen when the doorbell rang at exactly eight-thirty.

Oh, no! She erupted out of the kitchen before Bob could go to the door and said in an urgent whisper, 'If that's Rex Kynaston, tell him I'm not in.'

'Eh?' Bob looked startled. 'Is he calling for you, then?'

'He said he might, but I don't want to go out with him.'

The two men exchanged glances, and Bob went to the door while Harry flew upstairs to listen from the bedroom window.

'Hi, there.' Rex's easy deep tones held no surprise at having the door opened to him by a man. 'I've called to collect Harry.'

'Harry?'

'Yeah. Is she ready?'

'Er—um, I'm afraid Harriet isn't in,' Bob said pompously, and Harry remembered with annoyance that Bob always had been a rotten liar.

'Is that a fact?' There was a brief pause until Rex said firmly, 'In that case, I guess I'll just come in and wait until she gets back.' And Bob, like a complete fool, let him walk into the house with hardly a protest!

Now what was she supposed to do? Harry wondered fumingly. Stay trapped in the bedroom until Rex got fed up and went away, presumably. Below her she could hear the faint murmur of voices, as Rex greeted Eric and they started talking. Harry sat gingerly in a chair and realised that she was going to be very bored for a while because this wasn't even her bedroom, it was Eric's, and there was nothing for her to do except look out of the window at the street and think about Rex. What was he wearing? she wondered. And what on earth were the three men finding to talk about? They were even laughing now! Harry stirred restlessly, hating to be inactive. You'd think that Bob and Eric would have the sense to freeze Rex out, she thought, knowing that she was trapped up here. But then she realised, with a reluctant grin, that it was just the kind of situation that Bob and Eric would think a good joke, and they would probably try to keep Rex there as long as possible, on purpose.

Having resigned herself to a long wait, Harry was pleasantly surprised when she heard voices in the hall and then the front door open and close only half an hour or so later. But when she peeped out of the window her eyes widened in astonishment as she saw that it was Eric and Bob who were leaving! They grinned up at her maliciously and sauntered down the road in the direction of the pub.

Harry stood at the window, watching them go, wondering what to do, then she heard the door to the sitting-room open and Rex come out into the hall. 'Harry,' he called up. 'Are you going to come down here or do I have to come up and fetch you?'

For a moment she stood transfixed, then gave an inward groan and went out reluctantly on to the landing. Rex was waiting for her at the foot of the stairs, leaning casually against the banister, one foot on the bottom step. He looked up at her, his left eyebrow raised in mocking amusement, enjoying her discomfiture. 'Just how long were you willing to stay up there?' he asked sardonically.

'Just as long as it took you to get the message and leave. Did they tell you I was at home?' she asked, coming slowly down the stairs.

'They didn't have to—they thought it was too darn funny.'

She reached the bottom step and from there was able to look at him on the same level, eye to eye.

'I guess you weren't expecting me,' Rex said, taking in her jeans and T-shirt and the plastic Snoopy apron she'd put on to do the washing-up. 'But I always keep my word, honey. You should know that by now.'

Other promises—or rather threats—that he'd made came to her mind. That he wanted her and was determined to have her, for example. Harry's eyes widened, and she grew suddenly afraid as she looked into his intent face. Reaching out, Rex put a hand behind her neck, drew her down the last step and into his arms. For a long moment he gazed into her face, then bent hungrily to kiss her, his lips playing short havoc with her efforts to resist him.

He raised his head at last, again looking down into Harry's face, but oh, how different now! Where there had been doubt and fear, now there was only softness and desire, her eyes languid, her mouth pouting open in sexual awareness. Rex smiled and drew her into the sitting-room. He went to take her in his arms again, but she held back.

'Weren't you—curious,' she asked, 'to find that I was living with two men?'

'You mean, why wasn't I jealous?'

'You didn't even seem surprised.'

'I wasn't. I already knew about the set-up here.'

Harry frowned in puzzlement. 'But how could you have...?' Then her face cleared. 'Oh, of course, from Emma. Is that why you took her to the station?'

Rex nodded. 'I wanted to find out if there was some other man in your life. Emma told me that there were two—but I didn't have to worry about them.' Lifting up a hand, he began to gently stroke her face, his fingers touching her skin as lightly as a butterfly's wings as he explored her features caressingly. 'You know,' he said softly, 'you're really starting to get to me.'

Harriet almost said, I bet you say that to all the girls, but stopped herself, biting her lip and looking away from him.

His hand stilled. 'Harry?' She didn't answer, so he cupped her chin and forced her to look at him. 'What is it? Don't you believe me?'

'Should I?' she answered rather sardonically, and pulled away from him to go over to a table lamp and switch it on, dispelling the gathering, too intimate, dusk.

Coming up behind her, Rex put his hands on her shoulders. 'I wouldn't say it if I didn't mean it.' And he pushed aside her hair to kiss her neck, his lips sending a sudden delicious tremor of sensuousness coursing through her. Maybe Rex felt it, because his grip tightened and he moved closer so that she could feel the hardness of his body against her back. 'You caught my attention the first time I saw you,' he told her. 'You seemed so cold and distant, but when you flashed your eyes at me when you got angry... well, then I knew I had to get to know you better, find out if there really was fire underneath the ice.'

Slipping his hands beneath her arms, Rex stroked her breasts over the soft material of her shirt, then moved on down to caress her waist, moving inside so that his hands were on her bare skin.

'Turn around,' he murmured in her ear and, slowly, almost against her will, Harriet did so. There was no mockery or even triumph in his face now, only the lean hunger of desire. 'You're special, Harry. Very special.'

Raising her hands to put them on his shoulders, she said, 'Am I? Do you really mean that?'

'Yes, I do. Haven't I said so?'

'You have quite a reputation with women, Rex. For all I know, this is just a line.'

He had bent his head to kiss her neck, but now he looked up to study her troubled face for a moment before leading her to the settee. He sat down with her across his lap, and to feel Rex's body so close, to have his arm around her and his mouth within kissing distance, was heady stuff. Why was it, she wondered, that she should feel this blatant sexual need with one man, but not with another? What basic chemistry was it within her that caused a reaction like this? Almost, she resented it; she certainly resented this domination of her body over her mind, but had the terrible feeling that there wasn't a thing that she could do about it.

'Listen,' Rex was saying. 'I told you before that the Press exaggerate. I don't know what it's like over here, but in the States I only have to date a girl and it's reported in all the papers that she's my new romance, that we're either having an affair or we're contemplating marriage. Well, it just isn't so. I've——' he hesitated, 'seldom contemplated marriage with anyone, and a good half of the romances aren't true.'

She looked at him curiously. 'But you have contemplated it?' His face hardened and she said gently, 'What happened?'

Rex hesitated for so long that she thought he didn't care enough about her to tell her, and somehow it suddenly became very important that he should. At length, he began to speak and Harry had to quickly stifle a sigh of relief. 'A couple of years ago I really fell for a girl,' he admitted. 'She was an actress who'd come down from New York to try to break into television. We started going together, and then she asked me to get her a part in my series,' Rex added, his voice slowing. Then it took on a bitter note. 'When she found out that I had no say in who appeared, she left me for the casting director, who most certainly did.'

Harry looked at him sharply. 'You offered to help me get a part in your series.' She sat up. 'I thought at the time it was some sort of test and I was right, wasn't I?'

She moved to get off his lap, but Rex held her back. 'Yes, it was. Listen, try to understand. There are thousands of young actresses in the States all looking for the big break. They think that by getting to know people already in televison it will help them to get a part. Well,

I'm tired to death of being chased by girls who are willing to do just about anything to get what they want. So now, if I'm interested in a girl, I offer first to see what the reaction is.'

'And did I pass your test?' Harry demanded, her voice brittle.

'You know you did. But I don't think I passed yours, did I?'

'What do you mean?'

'You said that there were reasons you were antagonistic towards me before we even met, but you haven't told me what they are.'

Harry hesitated, but realised that not to tell him would be unfair, after all he had confided in her. So she told him about the last film she'd been in and of the big star who had ruined it and had tried to use sexual coercion.

'Was he English or American?' Rex demanded. But before she could answer, 'Did you have to go to bed with him?'

'No, I did not,' Harry snapped back. 'Any more than I have to go to bed with you.' And again she tried to get off his lap.

Grabbing her wrist, Rex held her still and smiled at her. 'But there's a difference—you *want* to go to bed with me. And even though I automatically set you that stupid test, I knew even then that you were special, that I wanted you very, very much.' And leaning forward he gave her a long, sensuous kiss.

He let her go and she opened her eyes to sigh and tilt her head to study his face. 'OK, I suppose I'll just have to believe you.'

'You make it sound as if you don't want to.'

'Maybe I don't. I've an idea that life will be a lot less complicated if I just told you to get lost here and now.'

'Nothing's going to get complicated,' he soothed. 'Because you feel the same way as I do. Don't you? Don't you?' he insisted.

Harry sighed again. 'I have to admit that you do have the strangest effect on my insides. Do you have this effect on all the women you meet?'

'Most of them,' Rex agreed complacently.

'You heel!' She punched him in the ribs. 'You ought to be the last man I'd ever...' She bit off the last words.

'Ever what?' Rex prompted. 'Come on, tell me.'

'No, you're too darned conceited already.'

'Ever fall for—is that what you were going to say?' Harriet didn't deny it and he smiled. 'Don't fight it, honey. You may even get to like it.' And putting a hand in her hair, he lifted her head until their mouths were almost touching. 'You're beautiful, Harry,' he said softly. 'Do you have any idea how much I want you?' he questioned thickly and kissed her with urgent hunger.

'I'm beginning to get the message,' she answered breathlessly, when he at last raised his head a few minutes later.

'Can't you ever be serious?' he said in sudden anger. 'Maybe you'll get this message a little better.' Laying her back against the arm of the settee, Rex kissed her with a fierce passion that crushed her lips under his. She gasped, her mouth opening under the onslaught of his kiss, and her hands went round his neck.

'Rex...' She said his name on a long sigh, as his hands slid inside her shirt, hot on her skin. He buried his head in her neck, his mouth tracing scorching kisses along the column of her throat, and bit the lobe of her ear. Her breath caught in her throat and Harry tried to pull away, unable to bear the sensuous emotions it aroused in her.

Lifting his head, Rex looked down at her flushed face and pouting lips. 'Take this off,' he ordered, touching her shirt. 'I want to look at you.'

She stared at him for a moment, half resenting and half excited by this order to strip. Her lips hovered on the brink of a curt refusal, but then she slowly sat up and pulled the T-shirt over her head. She looked at him rather defiantly, but after a long moment capitulated to the dark desire in his eyes and reached to the front of her bra to unhook it, slowly part the lacy fabric and then slip it off her shoulders.

Rex gently cupped her breasts in his hands, his eyes caressing her. 'You're lovely. Perfect,' he said sincerely, his thumbs circling her already proud nipples.

She gave a little gasping moan as he toyed with her, and put her hands on his shoulders, her nails digging into him. He kissed her then, with the fierce need of frustration, his hands still fondling her breasts, but then his mouth abruptly left hers to take the place of his hand, his lips driving her crazy. Putting her hands in his hair, she held his head against her breast, her body arching to meet him. 'Rex! Oh, God, Rex.' His lips sucked hard at her nipple and she gave a bitten-off cry.

'*Now* do you get the message?' Rex asked fiercely as he lifted his head away.

'Yes, oh, *yes*.'

'Then say it,' he demanded forcefully.

'I—I want you,' she admitted hoarsely, and saw the gleam of triumph in his eyes at her surrender.

He stood up and pulled her to her feet. 'Where's your room?'

But Harriet hadn't lost her senses that completely. She shook her head. 'No, not here. Bob and Eric will be home soon and anyway...'

'OK, get dressed and we'll go back to my flat.'

But again she shook her head. 'Not there, either.'

Catching hold of her arms, Rex said angrily, 'What is this, some kind of a tease? I don't like girls who play games, Harry. Not now. Not at this stage.'

'I'm—I'm not playing games, Rex.' With trembling hands she picked up her shirt, but Rex pulled it out of her hands and threw it on the floor. 'I'm *not*,' she said urgently. 'I've already told you that I don't sleep around. If I go to bed with you, then—then I want it to really mean something. I want to care about you and—and respect you. And I want you to feel the same way about me. And there's a porter at your block of flats; if I go back with you he might phone the newspapers. Tell them about us.' Lifting her arms she tried to cover her breasts from his gaze, embarrassed to be standing there like that, but he angrily pulled them down, holding her wrists in one of his hands and with the other starting to fondle her again.

'So what?' he said vehemently, his fingers doing sensational things to her nipples. 'Why the hell should we care that everyone knows?'

She pulled herself sharply away from him, hardly able to think straight and knowing that she was close to giving in. 'Rex, I have a family. How do you think they're going to feel if they read in the newspapers that their only daughter is having an affair with a man with your kind of reputation? I have to think of their feelings, of what it will be like for them with all their neighbours and friends knowing. No, Rex, I'm not going to do it.'

He grew still, staring at her. 'So what the hell are you saying?'

'That I'd like some more time. I—I want to be sure before I lay myself open to that kind of gossip.'

'Sure of what?' Rex demanded tersely, his jaw still set.

'That we're not going to get tired of each other after a couple of days. That just going to bed together isn't going to be all we have.'

'*Just* going to bed together?' Pulling her to him, Rex kissed her again, his face relaxing. 'It's going to take me a long time before I get tired of you, honey. How many times do I have to tell you that?'

Smiling a little, Harry put her arms around his neck. 'I'm sorry, but I need convincing.' Then she looked at him provocatively, enjoying her power over him. 'Don't you think it will be worth waiting—just a little?'

He made a sound deep in his throat, his arms tightening around her. 'Is that what this was, a trailer for the big feature? Yeah, I think it's worth the box-office money. So we'll try it your way. But boy, honey, I'm going to be frustrated as hell until we can get together.' He kissed her, his hands again caressing her. 'But make it soon, Harry. We're only wasting precious time. Time when we could be close like this. And even closer.'

His hands and lips began their insidious magic all over again, but Harry determinedly pushed him away, her breathing unsteady. 'No, Rex, you promised.'

For a moment it seemed as if he wasn't going to take no for an answer again, but then he nodded and stepped back reluctantly. 'OK,' he sighed. 'But this is a hell of a waste.'

When he'd gone, Harry stayed up long enough to tell Bob and Eric, who came home shortly afterwards, just what she thought of them, and then went up to bed. She did so feeling slightly giddy at her own rashness, but it was a heady, exciting madness, one that made her pulses race and her body come alive as it had never done before. There was a vitality about Rex that she found exhilarating, and it struck an answering chord in herself. And there was an audacious masterliness about him, too, that few men had. In the morning, she knew, she would probably regret what she'd done; things always seemed to lose their romantic glow in the cold light of day, but right now... Her thoughts went winging to the ceiling on a wave of high anticipation and desire, and she couldn't help but wonder how it would have been if she'd said yes and Rex had been with her in her bed now.

Almost as if in answer to her thoughts, the phone rang a short time later and she hastily picked up her bedside extension. 'Hello,' she said softly.

'Hi, there.' Rex's voice came clearly across the line, almost as if he was there beside her. 'You in bed?'

'Yes,' Harriet admitted, snuggling down into the pillow.

'I ought to be with you.'

Her lips curved into a delighted smile. 'I just knew that you were going to say that.'

'And weren't you thinking the same? Admit you were.'

Harry laughed. 'That way only leads to frustration.'

'It needn't,' Rex said meaningfully. 'But I admit I am very—very frustrated right now. You ought to be ashamed of yourself for leaving a guy like this.'

'Ah, I feel so sorry for you,' Harry mocked.

Rex laughed and said, 'You were so busy pushing me out of the door we forgot to make any plans for tomorrow. I have to appear in a children's television programme in the morning, but I thought maybe we could meet some place for lunch and then you could show me some of those tourist places you were telling me about.'

'OK, fine. Where shall I meet you?'

They arranged a time and place, and then Rex, his voice softening and becoming suggestive, said, 'What are you wearing in bed? Let me guess, I bet it's a slinky black nightdress with lots of lace on it.'

Harry laughed. 'Is that what your women usually wear?'

'I wish you wouldn't keep saying "your women" all the time. It makes it sound as if I have a house full of them back home. And I *haven't*,' Rex added quickly. 'That's before you can ask.'

'But you're not denying you have the opportunity?'

'The opportunity, perhaps, but not the inclination. There's a world of difference between the two, Harry. I don't want every girl I meet.'

'But those you do want, you take.'

'I want *you*,' he emphasised, squashing what might have led to a quarrel. 'You have a great figure, did you know that? I bet your body's beautiful. What I've seen certainly is, and I can't wait to see the rest. Don't keep me waiting too long, Harry. Not when you've already said that you want me.'

'Did I say that?' Harry teased. 'I must have been out of my mind.'

'On the contrary, you were yielding to the inevitable. Because what's going to happen between us is inevitable, Harry, don't you feel that?'

'Yes. Yes, I suppose I do,' she admitted on a sigh.

'It was bound to happen from the moment we met. We struck sparks. That doesn't often happen, not to me, anyway. So why don't we enjoy what we have, honey? That's what we both want, isn't it?'

His voice was softly insinuating and persuasive, but Harry wished that she could see his face. After hesitating a moment, she said, 'Rex, I'm not very... I mean, this isn't an easy thing for me to do.'

'Sure, honey, I know.' But then his voice grew mocking, and it was obvious that he didn't believe her. 'Are you trying to tell me you're a virgin?'

Her only defence was flippancy, as Harriet said drawlingly, 'Why, sure! Didn't you know? I'm part of the late twentieth-century Puritan backlash.'

Rex chuckled, his voice richly masculine over the phone. 'Then I guess I'll just have to use all my American know-how to make you unfreeze. Although for a Puritan you were pretty hot tonight. I'm really looking forward to going to bed with you, Harry. And I want you to move in with me.'

'Move in with you?' Harriet hadn't expected that he would want to commit himself that far.

'That's right. I want you with me, sweetheart—all the time. OK?'

Her voice a little choked, Harriet stammered, 'OK. I'll—I'll think it over. See you tomorrow. Goodnight.'

'Goodnight, sweetheart,' he breathed, and her skin prickled as she almost felt his closeness.

Slowly Harry replaced the receiver, then lay looking up at the ceiling for a long moment before reaching to turn off the bedside light and go to sleep.

He took her to the Savoy Grill for lunch. Harriet had been taken there before, but it wasn't a place she knew well or particularly liked. Mostly, she had gone there with men who had been trying to impress her—or get her to go to bed with them, she thought wryly as she got out of the limo that Rex had sent to pick her up. She nodded to the doorman and walked straight to the bar where Rex was waiting for her. Harriet paused in the doorway, tall and poised in a cream summer suit, her dark hair a shining crown to her lovely face. There was a pause in the hubbub of conversation as nearly every male head in the place turned to let their eyes travel over her, some of their faces appreciative and admiring, others simply lascivious.

Ignoring them all, Harry walked across the room to a small table in the far corner where Rex had risen to his feet, so tall that she could see him easily over the crowd. Eyes followed her as she went up to him, and became frankly envious as Rex put his hand on her waist, drew her to him and kissed her possessively.

'Hi,' he said to her with a wicked grin when he let her go.

'Good afternoon,' Harriet answered coolly. 'I see you're on your usual form.'

He laughed and pulled out a chair for her. 'What would you like to drink?' he asked, beckoning the waiter. They ordered and Rex looked her over appreciatively. 'You look very lovely this morning. And relaxed, too.'

'It's my day off. I don't have to worry about the film,' Harry replied lightly, but it wasn't strictly true. She felt much more at ease with Rex now, and could enjoy his company without feeling so tense and nervous. He had promised to give her time and, although this might be sexually frustrating for both of them, it also relieved the pressure. And the fact that he had confided in her about his ex-girlfriend had made Harry feel far more secure and self-confident. Rex didn't seem such an over-powering stranger now. He, too, was human, had fallen for the wrong girl and lost her to ambition. And it proved that he was capable of deeper feelings, because it had left him bitter and distrusting. Well, maybe this respite that he had promised would give her time to convince him that she at least could be trusted and he would feel deeply for her as well. Harry certainly hoped so.

Glancing up, she met his eyes, eyes that sent a very definite message, but were warm too, and her heart lurched almost as much as it had when she'd walked into the bar and seen him across the room. She gave a small smile and turned back to her drink, her thoughts in chaos. Oh, lord, I'm falling in love with him, was para-mount. But it's too soon, much too soon. I hardly know him. And yet in some ways she felt as if she had always known him, that he had always been there, deep in her heart. Unable to resist, Harry turned to look at him again and found his eyes still on her. Rex smiled, that special smile that made her heart flip over, then he put his hand out to cover hers, stroking it, his thumb gently but firmly probing between her fingers, a sensation that was strangely but fantastically sensuous.

It brought sexual tension flooding back, and to break it Harry took her hand away and said in a slightly ragged tone, 'How does filming in England compare with America?'

Rex grinned, enjoying her discomfiture, knowing full well the effect he was having on her. But he accepted the change of tempo and said, 'You sound just like a television interviewer.' Settling back in his chair, he went on, 'I haven't made many cinema films, only a few bit parts before I got the television role. This is my first lead in a film and I was really looking forward to it. And of course it means a lot to me.'

'Wouldn't you rather have made your first big film in America? On your home ground, so to speak?'

Rex shook his dark head. 'Not necessarily. I'd heard a lot about British directors and film-makers. How good and professional they were. And I certainly found everyone very friendly and helpful—with one notable exception,' he added after a very deliberate pause.

Harry had the grace to colour slightly, but said, 'I understand that you—or your agent—drove a very hard bargain when it came to percentage of the box office receipts and salary.'

Catching the hardening note in her voice, Rex's eyebrows rose. 'If I'm not mistaken, that's another thing you're holding against me?'

'I just think that a lot more films could be made if famous actors didn't demand so much money. Stars, producers, directors, the studios, they all seem to want their cut.'

Rex nodded. 'Yeah, it's a cut-throat business all right. But it's difficult for well known actors. It's like this: if an actor's in a film and it's a hit then he can demand a big percentage of the next film, but if that's a flop then his percentage goes right down again. You're always only as good as your last film or television show, and often actors don't last very long, so you have to make as much as you can while you're on top.'

It was an interesting argument, and one that Harry hadn't really considered before. They discussed it at more length, and Harry found that yet another of her preconceived ideas about Rex had been wrong and the barrier no longer existed.

They had a leisurely lunch, talking a lot and finding that they had far more in common than Harry had thought possible: books, the history of the cinema, an enthusiasm for cars. They even shared the same taste in wine, both enjoying the dry red wines of the Saint Emilion area. Afterwards, they did all the usual tourist places: the Tower, Buckingham Palace, and Trafalgar Square, where Harriet took Rex's photo as he stood with his arms outstretched and pigeons perched all over him, even on his head. She took her time over taking the photo, hoping that one of the pigeons might use the traditional method to bring Rex luck, but he must have had a charmed life, because he got away with it and she had to eventually take the snap.

Taking the camera from her, Rex said, 'OK, now it's your turn.' He grinned maliciously. 'Maybe I'll have better luck than you did.'

Harry laughed. 'You guessed, huh?'

'Mm.' Putting his arm round her he pulled her close against his side and pretended to hold his fist against her face. 'You'd just better watch it, woman, or I could get real nasty.'

Wrinkling her nose up at him, Harry retorted, 'Pooh, I'm not afraid of you!' And she parted her lips to impishly poke her tongue at him just a little.

Immediately his grip tightened fiercely. 'God, Harry, you're so damn sexy. Most of the time you're so cool and untouchable, but then you do something like that, that's so tantalising that you turn me on right here in Trafalgar Square! Jeez, Harry, I'm getting so damn hungry for you. If we don't do something about it soon I'll...'

Harriet looked alarmed. 'Not right here and now, I hope,' she broke in.

Rex roared with laughter. 'Almost, sweetheart. Almost.' He smiled down at her. 'And you make me laugh a lot, too. I like that.'

But he wasn't the only one who was laughing. Nearby a group of schoolgirls had recognised him and were standing giggling as they watched him.

'Oh-oh. I think we'd better make a run for it before we're surrounded,' he advised, and they hurried back to the waiting limo.

The chauffeur drove them on to see St Paul's Cathedral and the other sights of the original ancient City of London, the 'square mile' as all Londoners called it. Rex did things in style; making the car wait while they got out to explore and take photographs. And he did things in style, too, that evening, when he took her out to dinner and then on to a nightclub, finishing up at a casino where he played roulette. Harriet had gone home to change into a long dress speckled with black sequins that caught the light when they danced. It was her most expensive and flattering dress, and Harry knew that she looked good in it without seeing the way Rex's eyes lit up when he called to pick her up. He brought her flowers, too, and some expensive perfume that was all the rage in London.

At the restaurant they held hands a lot and were very close, and over dinner Harry told him about her family; her two brothers who spent most of their spare time renovating old cars, her mother who devoted most of her days to voluntary work, and her father who was a respected country solicitor.

After she'd explained that a solicitor was the English name for a lawyer, Rex said, 'So you're telling me that your family are respectable. Would they be shocked if you came to live with me?'

Harry gave a small sigh. 'Not shocked, I suppose, in this day and age. But they certainly wouldn't like it. Especially if it was common knowledge.'

'So what *are* you saying?' Rex demanded, his voice hardening. 'That it's OK for us to be together, so long as no one knows about it? That the only reason you're holding out on me is because you're afraid of what your family's neighbours might think?'

'No,' Harry began to protest in consternation. 'It isn't like that at all. I . . .'

'Then just how is it? Just what is there to wait for, Harry?'

'You promised to give me some time.'

'But how long, for God's sake? What difference is it going to make if we go to bed together tonight or in a week's time? It certainly won't make any difference to me.' His hand gripped hers tightly. 'I want you *now*, Harry. And I want you bad.'

'For heaven's sake! Keep you voice down.'

'Why? I'm not ashamed of wanting you. But it sure as hell seems as if you're afraid of committing yourself to me.'

Harry got abruptly to her feet and picked up her evening bag. 'Excuse me.'

Looking up, Rex saw her stony face and half rose out of his chair. 'Harry, wait. I didn't mean... Oh, hell!' he muttered, as she avoided his outstretched arm and walked quickly away from him and made for the door, her head high and her back rigid with anger.

CHAPTER SIX

INSTEAD of marching straight out of the nightclub as she'd first intended, Harry hesitated for a second in the entrance and then walked into the ladies' cloakroom. Once there, she found that her hands were shaking with anger and she had to grip her bag tightly. Damn the man! How dared he speak to her like that? And in a public place, too! Did he really think that she was going to capitulate, just because they'd spent the day together? Did spending the day with him mean that she'd got to spend the night, too? Harry wondered with bitter cynicism. Well, that might be how he behaved with his other women, but it certainly wasn't going to work with her. Taking a lipstick from her bag, Harry went to put some on, but her hands were still shaking so much that she had to force herself to calm down.

When she'd applied the lipstick, Harry stepped back and was about to turn away, when she caught a glimpse of herself in the mirror and stopped. So often when you looked in the mirror, you only saw a small part of yourself, very seldom taking time to study the complete picture. But Harry tried to see herself now as Rex must see her. Tall, slender, poised, dressed very sophisticatedly and her lovely face made-up to stunning effect. Hardly surprising, then, that he thought her far more experienced and worldly than she actually was. For a few seconds she felt angry again, because he didn't realise, because he hadn't that much insight. But then she saw that she was doing him an injustice; Rex really couldn't be expected to know, he could only go by his own experiences with other far more willing and available girls. Harry didn't much like the idea of being put on a par with that kind of girl, and she couldn't see how they could develop any kind of a close relationship if Rex thought of her on that level.

She ought, she knew, to walk away from him. To walk away from it *now*, before she fell really deeply in love with him and got terribly hurt. Oh, hell! Harriet pulled out a small comb from her bag and pulled it forcefully through her hair, then stopped, gazing at her unhappy-eyed face in the mirror. For a few minutes common sense warred with emotion, and then her shoulders straightened and her chin came up determinedly. Harriet had always been a fighter, and she was darned if she was going to turn her back and walk away from the most emotionally exciting relationship she'd ever had with a man, just because she was afraid of getting hurt. Not when there was even a remote chance of it developing into something more than just a sexual affair. They would just *have* to get to know one another better so that their romance—affair, whatever you cared to call it—would have a chance to grow. Somehow she would have to convince him that she wasn't the same as all those other girls.

Resolutely, she pushed open the door of the ladies' room and walked out into the hallway. Rex was waiting for her. He was leaning against the wall, his hands in his pockets, trying not to look like a man who was impatiently waiting for his girl. He straightened up as soon as he saw her, his eyes fixed intently on her face. And it was that almost anxious look that dispelled the last of Harry's anger. His face clearing, Rex stepped forward and took a firm hold of her arm, as if making sure that she couldn't leave his side again.

'Let's go on some place else,' he said tersely.

They didn't speak again until they were seated in the back of the limo, leaning back against the soft leather upholstery. Putting his arm round her, Rex drew her close to him. 'For a minute there, I thought you'd walked out on me,' he said in a low tone, so that the driver couldn't hear.

'For a minute there, I nearly did,' Harriet told him wryly.

'What made you change your mind?'

She shrugged and shook her head, unwilling to answer.

'Could it have been this?' Rex asked softly and pushed her hair aside to kiss her neck, his lips sensuously soft against her skin. 'Could it?' he insisted, his mouth playing havoc with her senses.

Slowly she turned her head to look at him, this man who had the power to make her forget everything else but the physical need she felt for him when he was near; who could make nonsense of reality, and common sense fly out of the window whenever he touched her. But was he a man who wanted only the use of her body until he tired of her? Her mind rebelled against the thought; there had to be something more, there *had* to be! But even though her mind was filled with this yearning wish, she still said flippantly, 'What else?' and leaned forward so that he could kiss her on the mouth.

At the nightclub they danced between each act in the cabaret. Rex held her close, confident again of the power he held over her, his hands low on her waist as they danced, his eyes looking suggestively down into hers. Someone took their photograph and he hardly blinked.

He obligingly signed his autograph for a few women, but when a quite well known columnist came up and tried to talk to them, probing to find out Harriet's name, Rex abruptly told him to get lost.

'He'll be sure to find out my name, anyway,' Harriet pointed out. 'Don't you remember those publicity photos we had taken when you arrived in England?'

'Sure, but at least he won't have found out from me,' Rex said roughly, giving her a very direct look.

Harriet flushed, remembering their row earlier. It was such a shame that that had happened. They had been getting on so well and finding so much that they had in common that she had really begun to believe that they could be friends as well as lovers. 'Tell me about your family,' she said genuinely interested. 'Are any of them in show business, beside you?'

Rex shook his head and shrugged. 'No. They don't matter.'

'But I'd like to hear about them,' Harry protested.

'Why, so you can worry about what they might think? Well, you don't have to, they know that I'm a big boy now and what I do is no concern of theirs,' Rex said harshly.

Harry's face tightened at the sarcasm in his tone. 'Why are you being like this?'

Taking her hand Rex pulled her on to the dance-floor. 'I'll tell you why,' he said shortly, and pulled her hard against him, holding her there as they moved to the slow tempo of the music in the dimly lit room. 'Because I'm crazy about you,' he said fiercely in her ear. 'Because you look so damn lovely that you're driving me mad. When I see the way you walk I can hardly keep my hands off you, and when we dance together like this I can hardly stop myself from picking you up and taking you back to my flat, whether you want to go or not. That's why.' His hands tightened, almost hurting her. 'I don't know what it is about you . . .' He looked intently down into her face. 'So if this is just a game, Harry, if you're just playing hard to get . . .'

'I'm not,' she answered in little more than a whisper. 'But—but I want you to *care* about me, too.'

His jaw hardened as Rex said fiercely, 'I do care, honey. I really do.' And he buried his face in her neck to kiss her.

They didn't leave the nightclub until nearly two in the morning, but neither of them felt in the least tired, so they went on to a casino where Rex was instantly recognised and treated with due deference. He played at roulette for a while, but was no gambler, being more interested in turning to talk to Harriet as she stood behind him than in the play of the wheel, so after only about twenty minutes he stood up again.

'Would you like to play?' he asked her, holding out some chips.

Harry shook her head. 'No. Gambling doesn't do anything for me.'

He gave her a rather odd look and raised his eyebrows. 'You—are the strangest girl. Most women would jump at the chance to be staked at the roulette table.'

Tucking her hand into his arm, Harry said, 'I keep telling you—I'm not most women.'

Rex grinned and put his hand over hers. 'I'm beginning to believe you. Let's go and have supper.'

Harriet wasn't hungry, but there was no way she could resist the beautifully laid out cold buffet table in the restaurant opening off the gaming rooms. There were king prawns and lobster, smoked salmon and caviar, all the richest of foods for the richest of people who came to gamble and eat there.

They loaded up their plates and sat down to eat at a table tucked away in a corner. Rex ordered a bottle of champagne to go with the food and Harriet sipped it appreciatively. 'Mmm, delicious! This is really living,' she said with a contented sigh.

Smiling at her dreamy expression, Rex said, 'I wonder if that's how you'll look when we've made love?'

Her enjoyment spoiled, Harriet replied coldly, 'I wouldn't know.'

'You're mad at me,' Rex hazarded. 'Now why, I wonder? Don't tell me you're a prude, Harry.'

Tilting her head consideringly, she thought about it for a moment, then said, 'I rather think I must be. Remarks like that certainly don't turn me on, if that's what they're supposed to do.' Her voice was still cool and her expression was definitely withdrawn.

'You know, Harry, a guy could get frost-bite when you put on your cold-English-girl act.'

Her eyes lit with laughter, but then she said, 'Do you really think it's an act?'

'Isn't it?' Rex countered, his eyes resting lazily on her face.

'And is your dominant masculine image an act, too?' Harriet asked in return.

'I told you before, I save all my acting for the cameras. I dislike people who play at being a movie star when they're off the set.'

'And so do I,' Harry said firmly.

Rex's eyes went swiftly to her face and he looked at her for a long moment with a frown between his eyes, but then he shrugged. 'Well, at least you like the champagne.' And he refilled her glass. 'What shall we do tomorrow? More sightseeing?'

Harriet picked up her glass and looked at it as she shook her head. 'Sorry, I can't make tomorrow. I'm busy.'

Rex's face tightened. 'A date?' he asked coldly.

'Sort of,' Harry answered, her voice even. 'I'm going home to see my family.'

His face immediately relaxed. 'I see.' He looked at her persuasively. 'Couldn't you skip it for once? Tell them you've got to take pity on a poor foreigner who doesn't know anyone else.' And he reached out to take hold of her hand.

'*Got* to?' Harry asked, her eyebrows raised.

'Want to, then.' And he gave her that crinkly-eyed smile.

But Harriet shook her head. 'The temptation is, of course, almost irresistible, but no, sorry.'

'We could come here again,' Rex cajoled. 'You could have some more of that lobster.'

Laughing delightedly, Harriet said, 'Now, that is really putting temptation in a girl's way. But food like this is only a treat if you have it occasionally; to have it too often would make it commonplace. No, I'm afraid I have to go home.'

'OK.' Rex nodded disappointedly and picked up his glass, turned a little away from her to look across the room at a group of people who had just come into the supper-room.

For a moment Harry studied his profile, then said slowly, 'Of course, you could always come with me tomorrow, if you would care to.'

She saw his lips give a wry kind of twitch before he shook his head. 'Thanks, but I guess I'll do some sight-seeing on my own,' he said dismissively.

Harry sat back in her chair, feeling almost rebuffed. There had been no motive behind her invitation, although he obviously thought there was; she wasn't trying to trap him into anything by introducing him to her family, which was why she had hesitated before asking him. She had hoped that now he had admitted that he cared about her he would want to meet her family, but evidently he thought it too soon to commit himself that far. And maybe he was right. To break the feeling of constraint between them, she said lightly, 'Do you like old cars—really old ones, I mean?'

'I don't know much about them. But I'm very keen on sports cars. I have a Ferrari back home, but you're restricted to driving at fifty miles an hour now in the States. Before I got the part in the television series, I used to race cars, but I had to sign to say I wouldn't while I was under contract. But really old cars, I've never had much to do with.'

'That's a shame. My brothers and I are restoring a veteran car that we bought from a farmer who had left it to rot in his barn. We're hoping to finish it in time to take part in the London to Brighton.'

'The London to Brighton?' Rex asked, his interest aroused.

'It's a car rally. Only cars built in or before 1904 can take part.'

'And that's what you do on Sundays—work on an old wreck of a car?' Rex asked in amazement.

'Uh-huh. And I restored my Lotus with my own two hands.' And she held them out, palms upwards, expressively.

Taking them in his, Rex said, 'They're still soft.' He put both her hands in one of his and stroked them sensuously. 'I could think of much better things to do with your hands,' he said in erotic suggestion.

Harriet's breath caught in her throat and her hands trembled in his as a wave of physical need grew inside her.

His hands tightening convulsively at her reaction, Rex, his voice suddenly thick, said, 'There's only one way to end an evening like this, Harry. I want to take you to bed. Come back to my flat tonight.'

'No.' Harry drew back and tried to take her hands away, but Rex held on to them. 'Please, you promised.'

After a moment Rex nodded. 'Yeah, I guess I did, at that. I'm sorry. But you're driving me to desperation, Harry. Don't make me wait too long.'

Her eyes softened, but she didn't speak.

'OK, I get the message,' Rex said with resigned impatience. He glanced down at her plate. 'Had enough?'

'Mm. It was delicious. Thank you.'

'I'll take you home, then.'

They found the limo driver fast asleep in the back seat. 'It seems a shame to wake him,' Harry said sympathetically.

But Rex was far more practical. 'Nevertheless, that's what he's paid for. The film company wouldn't be at all happy if either of us got caught for drinking and driving.' And he hard-heartedly woke the man up.

They sat close together in the car, each vibrantly aware of the other. Rex's arm was around her and he held Harriet's left hand in his, but he didn't attempt to kiss her because kisses wouldn't have been enough. Also, they were both conscious of the driver, who kept looking in his rear-view mirror to see what they were doing.

When they reached her house, Harriet said rather unsteadily, 'Would you—er—like to come in for a nightcap?'

Rex squeezed her hand. 'Thanks.' As they got out of the car he said to the driver, 'I won't be long.'

Her heart racing, Harriet led the way into the sitting-room, then turned to Rex.

He strode straight up to her and took her in his arms, his mouth coming down on hers so fiercely that Harry gasped, her mouth opening under his. As he kissed her he moulded her to his body and pressed himself against her, sending an answering fire coursing through her veins.

'You witch! What the hell have you done to me?' Rex muttered. 'I lie awake at nights thinking about you. Wishing you were beside me. Thinking about what it will be like and driving myself mad with frustration.' His hands tightened hungrily. 'God, Harry, I can't wait to go to bed with you.' And he kissed her again, not content with her mouth, but kissing her eyes, her throat, the line of her jaw, in a fever of intense passion.

Harriet clung to him, returning his kisses when he touched her mouth, her head in a whirl and her body raging with a desire that was as urgent as his.

The clock in the hall struck four, and Rex reluctantly lifted his head. They were both trembling; Harry could feel it as he held her close against his chest. 'I don't want to leave you, honey,' Rex said roughly. 'It's going to be damned hard.'

'I know.' Putting up her hand, she felt the soft dew of perspiration on his face. She suddenly wanted to lick it off, to lick him all over. With a little gasp, she stepped away from him.

'What is it?'

'I—it's nothing. I—I never felt like this about anyone before.'

'Like what? Tell me.'

Her voice a little more than a whisper, Harry replied, 'I've—never *wanted* anyone so—so badly.'

'Oh, sweetheart.' Drawing her to him again, Rex gave her one last long, lingering kiss before tearing himself away. 'If I don't go now I'll never go, and to hell with everything else. No, don't come to the door. Goodnight, Harry. I'll see you on the lot on Monday.'

'Yes. Goodnight.' But Harriet followed him to the door. It was almost light now, and she wanted the driver to see that she was still fully dressed. She didn't want any more rumours circulating about them than there were already.

The car drove away and Harriet leaned against the door jamb, her legs feeling suddenly weak. Sliding her back down the jamb, she sat on the floor, staring after the car and wishing now that she hadn't let him go. Closing her eyes, she dug her nails hard into her palms, her body still trembling in awareness. The deepness of their passion for each other made her feel giddy, and almost frightened. As Harriet had told Rex, she had never experienced anything like this before, and now she knew that it was too late to turn back; she had gone over the edge and was already plunging down the steep, whirling helter-skelter slide, unable to stop or go back. But all helter-skelter rides came to an end, usually a sudden and sometimes a painful one. Harry stood up, feeling suddenly cold, but determinedly closing her mind to what the future might hold.

It was almost lunch time when she reached her family home, and although she worked on the car with her brothers all the afternoon, her mind wasn't on what she was doing, and she spent most of the time wishing that she had gone out with Rex, or better still that he had come home with her. They could have had fun working on the car together.

But any differences between them were completely forgotten when Harry arrived at the studios on Monday morning and found her dressing-room full of flowers.

'Now, I wonder who they could be from?' Emma asked teasingly as she came in.

Harriet laughed. 'Must be an unknown admirer; there isn't any card.'

'As if you need one. The whole studio knows that Rex is crazy about you.'

'But it was you he took to the station on Friday,' Harry pointed out.

'Yes, but only so that he could ask me about you. He wanted to know whether you had a boyfriend. And I thought he was going to jump down my throat when I told him you lived with two men—until I enlightened him about the sleeping arrangements, that is,' Emma added. She looked at Harry curiously. 'And do you feel the same way about him?'

'Of course,' Harry returned with a flippancy she didn't feel. 'Who wouldn't fall head over heels for Rex Kynaston?'

She and Rex stopped at a pub for a drink on the way home from the studios that night, but filming had gone on until after eight o'clock and both of them were tired and had lines to learn for the next day's shooting, so they parted at ten-thirty. The shooting schedule for the rest of that week was heavy, too, but they saw as much of each other as possible, sitting together in what was a comparatively quiet corner of the extremely busy and noisy film studio between takes, and always sitting next to each other in the studio cafeteria at lunch time, making no secret of the fact that they were attracted to each other.

On Friday evening, after a gruelling week's work, they went into a pub for a drink and Rex held out a slim jeweller's box to her.

Harry hesitated, her eyes going swiftly to his face. 'What is it?'

'Open it and see.'

Slowly, she took the box from him and opened it. Inside was a gold link bracelet, and attached to the bracelet was a charm in the shape of a heart. 'Rex, I can't.' She went to give the box back to him, but he stopped her.

'Wait. Look at it.' Slowly Harry lowered her eyes and looked at the golden chain and the little heart nestling against the velvet. 'Doesn't it mean anything to you?' Rex asked softly.

'The heart? You mean—you mean, you're giving me *your* heart? Oh, Rex!' Silly tears came to her eyes and Harry had to blink them away.

Slipping his arm round her waist, Rex leaned forward and kissed her ear. 'I'm crazy about you, honey,' he murmured so that she alone could hear. 'Don't you believe me?'

Looking into his dark, intent eyes, Harry could only think that he was telling her that he loved her. Her heart quickened, and there was such a lump in her chest that she could hardly speak, only say his name. 'Oh, Rex…Rex…' For a moment her emotions were so strong that they threatened to engulf her and she was on the verge of telling him that she loved him, but realised in time that this was neither the time nor the place.

Taking the bracelet from the box, Rex fastened it on her wrist, his fingers setting her skin on fire. 'Whenever you look at it,' Rex told her, 'I want you to remember me.'

Her heart lurched again, but Harry managed to smile and say, 'You're a difficult man to forget.'

'Good.' Rex grinned and gave her a small kiss on the nose. 'That's what I hoped.'

As she looked at him, Harry knew quite suddenly and certainly that there was nothing left to wait for. She was in love with him and wanted to be with him—for ever, if it worked out that way. But if it didn't … Well, he had said that he cared, and during the past week they had found much in common on which to base a lasting relationship. But over and above all was this intense physical attraction that had drawn them together despite their original differences. When you boiled it down they were just a man and a woman who badly wanted and needed each other, and out of that had come love, and from that would grow friendship and companionship. That knowledge brought a radiant light of happiness to Harry's face, and with it the certainty that it was right to yield to him now and that, despite all her earlier reservations, she would go and live with him.

Her feelings must have been clear in her face because Rex's eyes widened, became intent, eager. 'Harry?' The question was no more than a breath, but it meant so much.

Slowly, she nodded and tried to smile, but she was so full inside that she couldn't.

'Sweetheart!' Rex's arm tightened convulsively. 'You won't regret it, honey, I swear it.' He kissed her, right there in the pub, unable to contain his jubilance. 'Come on, let's go back to my place.'

He went to get to his feet, but Harry caught his hand. 'No, wait. Not—not tonight.'

'Harry!' Her name was a wealth of protest.

'Listen.' She licked lips suddenly gone dry. 'Do you still want me to—to move in with you?'

'You know I do,' he answered urgently.

'Then, really, don't you think it would be better if we waited till tomorrow? We're both tired and——' she blushed '—and I don't want to have to get up and leave you—even for a few hours, but I must collect my clothes from the house. And there's lots of things I have to do tomorrow.'

Rex groaned impatiently. 'Honey, all that can wait. It isn't important—*we* are.'

'I know, but I want to do it right.' Her beautiful, long-lashed eyes looked into his tenderly. 'I'll come to you tomorrow. I promise.'

He continued to argue with her, but Harry was adamant and, in the end, he had no choice but to give in. 'What time will you come, then?'

'I suppose I could be there by about five.'

He looked disappointed. 'No earlier?'

'No,' Harry answered with a shake of her head. 'Do you want me to buy any groceries or anything on the way?'

'No, I'll take care of all that. Just bring yourself.'

'And my clothes? Are you sure that you really want me to—to move in?' Harry asked, looking for reassurance.

He gave it in abundance. 'Of course I do. I told you, I want you with me. I want to wake up and find you beside me in the mornings.' For an instant he looked almost surprised at his own admission, but then a devilish glint came into his eyes as he said, 'But, as for your clothes, bring them if you must, but you certainly won't be needing them.'

Harriet gulped, aware again of what she was committing herself to, and wanting to run away and hide. Perhaps something of her feelings showed on her face, because Rex put his arm round her shoulders and smiled into her eyes, then bent to kiss her lightly on the mouth. She closed her eyes for a moment, savouring the soft touch of his lips against hers, remembering the passion he was capable of and her own response to it. In that moment she decided to stop worrying about the future, to put it out of her mind completely and just to live for the present, so that she could savour each day of happiness as it came. Opening her eyes, she smiled back at him. 'Till tomorrow, then,' she said softly.

Lifting his glass, Rex clinked it against hers in a toast that neither of them would ever forget. 'Till tomorrow,' he agreed, with a wealth of meaning in his tone.

* * *

Harry was late arriving at the flat the next day. She had been too keyed up to sleep the night before, and so had woken late this morning. And there had been so much to do. Clothes to collect from the cleaners, lots of cat food to be bought in case the boys forgot, her hair to be washed, and it was her turn to clean the kitchen and sitting-room. And there had also been the difficult task of telling Bob and Eric, who were almost more protective of her than her own family, which was saying something. In the end she had chickened out and had put her cases in the car when they were out of the way. But Emma she *had* to tell.

'I—er—I'll be moving out for a while,' she told the other girl after knocking and going into her bedroom.

Emma looked up from doing her nails and grinned. 'So tell me something I don't know. I was wondering how long it would be before you completely capitulated to Rex's charms.'

'Will you tell Bob and Eric for me?'

'Coward. Yes, of course I'll tell them.'

'And if any of my family phone up just tell them that I'm out and I'll call them back. Then ring me, would you? Here's the number.'

It was deceitful and Harry didn't like doing it, but she felt that she wanted time for her relationship with Rex to settle before she broke the news to her parents. She could only hope that the Press wouldn't get hold of the story until she was ready to tell her family.

She left soon after, but had difficulty finding a parking place near the flat, so it was gone six when she arrived. By now the more mundane tasks of the day had taken away a lot of the romance of last night. Harry was keyed up and nervous, afraid that she was making the biggest mistake of her life, and it took quite a lot of will-power to lift up her hand and ring the bell.

Rex opened the door at once and almost pulled her inside. 'What happened to you?' he asked sharply. 'You said you'd be here by five.'

'There isn't anywhere to park near here,' Harry snapped back hotly. 'I had to leave most of my luggage because it was too far to carry it and I...'

Her words were broken off abruptly as Rex impatiently caught hold of her and pulled her into his arms. 'Shut up,' he said fiercely. 'Just shut up, will you?' Putting a hand on either side of her head, he silenced her with his mouth, holding her captive as he kissed her with a hunger that was almost savage in its intensity. Then he stooped and picked her up, carrying her into the bedroom and shouldering the door shut behind him.

The room was dominated by a huge bed. It was at least six feet wide, with a brass headrail and a snowy white coverlet. The room, too, was large, with one entire wall covered with mirror-fronted wardrobes. But Harry had no time to look further before Rex crossed to the bed and laid her down on it. 'So now I've got you where I want you, at last,' he said triumphantly. 'Where you belong.'

For a moment he continued to look down at her, the glint of anticipation in his eyes as they lingered over her slim figure, then he bent to take off her shoes before kicking off his own and lying down beside her. 'Hi,' he said softly, the tension of waiting gone now. 'I was starting to get worried.' Lying on his side, he put a hand on her thigh and began to gently caress her.

'That I wouldn't come?'

'No, that maybe you'd had an accident driving that crazy car of yours.'

'But you were sure that I'd come here; that I wouldn't have changed my mind. Oh, the egotism of the man,' Harry said, only half mockingly.

Rex grinned, but his hand tightened on her thigh. 'If you hadn't arrived when you did I would have gone over to your place and got you,' he said, with such forcefulness that Harry really believed he would have done.

Lifting her hand, she put it on his arm and felt the strength of his muscles through the thin material of his shirt. He was certainly strong enough to have carried her off by force if he'd wanted to. 'But I'm here now,' she reminded him, her voice low and unintentionally seductive.

'Yes.' Desire darkened his eyes and Rex put a hand up to gently stroke her face before bending to kiss her. He did so lingeringly, as if he had all the time in the world, taking her mouth in a sensuous, exploring kiss that made her feel as if she was drowning in a sea of pleasure and contentment. 'You're beautiful, honey,' he murmured against her mouth. 'So lovely.' His hand moved over her, slowly and caressingly, in no hurry now that he knew she was his for the taking. 'We're going to make love the whole weekend,' he told her, his lips moving across hers in little, biting kisses. 'I don't think I'm ever going to have enough of your body, sweetheart. You're so lovely. Perfect.' And his hand went to the buttons of her blouse and began to undo them.

Harry opened her eyes and looked up at this man who was about to become her lover, who was going to take off her clothes and look at her naked body, to touch and handle her as he pleased. And then was going to take her and use her to satisfy his physical needs.

And she wanted that as much as he, her reason and morality seduced by the irresistible need to be held in his arms and loved, by the deep yearning ache of emptiness inside her wanting to be filled by him—and only him. Modesty and innocence alike were as nothing compared to the strength of desire. So Harriet reached up to put her arms round his neck, to bring his head down so that she could kiss him with intense, impatient fervour.

Her kiss aroused Rex to an answering passion, but it was he who drew away first, his breathing uneven. 'Why, babe,' he said with surprised pleasure. 'This is really going to be some night.'

'Don't call me that,' Harry said sharply, feeling insecure again. 'Call me by my name.' She at least wanted him to be sure that it was *her* he was making love to, and not just another female body.

Frowning, Rex lifted his head to look at her, but then a slow smile came into his eyes. For a few minutes he was busy taking off some of her clothes, his hands adept at the task, then he lowered himself to half lie on top of her and began to kiss her. First he kissed her eyes, murmuring her name as he did so. 'Harry, my sweet Harry, you have such beautiful eyes. And your nose is exquisite, Harry,' he told her as he kissed it. 'And, my darling Harriet, such ears. I want to bite them like this, Harry, to make you wriggle and squirm the way you are now.' His lips moved slowly on. 'And such a perfect mouth, Harry, my darling. Sometimes so hot that you drive me wild, and sometimes so cold that you freeze my blood to ice. Oh, Harry, Harry, your chin, your throat.' His lips moved on down the column of her throat as he repeated her name over and over again, telling her how beautiful she was every inch of the way. Already her blood was on fire, but Harry's breathing grew shallow with almost unbearable anticipation as his lips reached her breasts.

'Oh, my gorgeous, beautiful girl,' he whispered softly. 'Oh, Harry, what lovely breasts you have. I want to touch them and hold them. Like this. And I want to take those little rosebud nipples in my mouth. Like this. Oh, Harry, how you moan when I do that to you? Can you like it, I wonder? And when I do *this* to them? No, don't fight to get away. You must learn to bear it, my darling Harriet, because I'm going to do it again and again.'

She cried out as his mouth pulled and squeezed, the intensity of pleasure almost more than she could endure. Her hands trembled on his shoulders, at once pushing him away and holding him back. Her breath was one long gasp and her hair clung damply to her forehead. At last, Rex let her go and raised himself so that his head was beside hers. 'Do you still think I don't know your name?' he demanded raggedly.

'No.' She stared up at him with wonder and a kind of humility in her eyes, all her doubts dissolved beneath his eagerness. She loved him so much, and to be loved in return made everything perfect. 'Oh, Rex!'

She buried her head in his shoulder, feeling suddenly shy again, and he held her like that until her breathing had become even and her heart was more or less back to normal. Then he lifted her head so that he could look at her flushed face and smiled. 'Why don't we have some champagne?' he suggested. 'I've got some on ice in the kitchen.'

Harriet nodded gratefully. 'That would be nice.'

Rolling off the bed, Rex put up a hand to straighten his hair while Harry looked round for her blouse and began to put it back on. His voice amused, Rex leaned down to kiss her again and said, 'Modesty has no place in our bedroom, honey.' And he deliberately pushed the front of her blouse aside so that he could touch her.

He did it so arrogantly that Harry immediately blushed, which made Rex laugh delightedly. 'Not many actresses can do that. Stay where you are; I'll get the champagne.'

A shadow flickered across Harry's eyes; did he really think she was acting at a time like this? But no, that couldn't be; it was only a passing remark. She felt secure and supremely happy now that she had committed herself at last, the future stretching ahead, full of love and companionship. She began to wander round the flat, looking into the bathroom that opened off the bedroom, which had a bath that was so wide you could easily get two people in it, even if one of them was as big as Rex. She flushed again, turned on by the pictures this conjured up, and moved into the sitting-room. This had two windows overlooking a garden at the back of the building and was comfortably furnished with a big settee and coffee-table, a television set, and with a dining-room suite and cupboards set into the shorter arm of the L-shaped room.

'It's a lovely flat,' Harry called out.

'Glad you like it,' Rex answered above the noise of ice being shaken into a bucket.'

'Is your place in America as big as this? Will there be enough room there for both of us?'

Rex came out of the kitchen and stood in the doorway with the ice-bucket in his hands. 'Sorry, what did you say?'

Smiling, Harry went over to him and put her arms round his neck to kiss him. 'Your place in America—will it be big enough for the two of us?'

He began to bend his head to kiss her, his eyes smiling, but as she watched him the smile died, his eyes becoming almost wary. 'Are you—thinking of going out there?'

'Why yes, of course. When the film's finished, and we go back there to live.' She added, 'I just hope my parents aren't too unhappy about it.'

Walking over to the drinks table, Rex set the bucket down. 'I thought you said you were going to audition for Stratford afterwards?' he said, with his back to her as he opened the champagne.

'Why, yes. But that was before—before this happened.' Going up behind him Harry put her arms round his waist and leaned her head against his broad back. 'Before we decided to live together.'

Putting down the champagne, Rex loosened her hands and turned round to face her, holding her a little away from him. Harry happily tilted her head to look at him, but her eyes widened when she saw his set face. 'What is it?'

'Let's get one thing straight right from the start, Harry. This set-up isn't meant to be for keeps. We'll stay together while I'm in England but, when the film is finished, then we'll split and I'll go back to the States—alone.'

CHAPTER SEVEN

HARRY stared at him, feeling suddenly numb and lifeless. 'What—what did you say?'

'I'm sorry, honey, but I just don't make that kind of promise.'

'But you—you asked me to come and live with you.' Harry's throat was so dry that she found it difficult to get the words out.

'Sure, while I'm over here.'

But her bemused brain couldn't believe it and she said gropingly, 'You said that you wanted me with you.'

'I do, honey, I do.' Rex put his hands on her shoulders, saying persuasively, 'I told you, sweetheart, I'm crazy about you—but coming back to the States with me just wouldn't work out. You don't want to give up your career, do you? And I sure wouldn't want you to, but you might find it hard to find work in America. And I'd be working all the time, and...'

Harry suddenly stepped back and knocked his hands off her shoulders. 'Get away from me! Don't touch me!' She glared at him, fierce anger replacing the shocked numbness. 'You're just making lame excuses. Why don't you say what you really mean?' she demanded hotly. 'You're not in love with me at all.'

Rex's face hardened, grew cold. 'I've never said that I was.'

'No, not in so many words, maybe. But just what was *this* supposed to mean, then?' And she jerked her wrist towards him, showing him the bracelet with the tiny heart dangling from it.

'It's a present, that's all.'

'That wasn't how I read it, and you know it! I thought it was a way of saying that you were in love with me. But obviously I was wrong,' she added, looking at his grim face. She gave a high-pitched, unnatural laugh and began to fumble with the catch of the bracelet.

'So just what are *you* saying?' Rex asked harshly. 'That you only came here because you believed I was in love with you?'

'Yes. Just that.'

'Then you're a liar, Harry. To yourself.' Stepping forward Rex caught hold of her arm. 'You came here because you wanted the same thing I do—to go to bed together. No matter how much you dress it up, that's what it boils down to.'

'No! You're wrong. I came because——' her voice faltered '—because I was stupid enough to fall in love with you.' For a moment her eyes looked pleadingly up into his, her heart yearning for her admission to soften his hardness, but if anything Rex's face became even more withdrawn, his mouth twisting grimly. Wrenching free of his hold, Harry at last managed to unclasp the bracelet and pulled it off, throwing it at his feet. 'Take back your damn present, then! If it means nothing to you, it most certainly means nothing to me!'

Becoming aware that she was only half dressed, she ran back into the bedroom and began to hurriedly pull on the rest of her clothes.

'Harry, wait. Now just wait a minute.' Rex tried to reach out for her, but she flung his hand aside, angrily pushing her blouse back into her skirt.

'I should never have come here,' she said bitterly, hurt pride wanting to make her hit back. 'I should have trusted my first judgement of you; I thought then that you were just a two-bit ham actor with nothing behind the pseudo-macho façade.' Straightening up from putting on her shoes, she said fiercely, 'You're just a sham, Rex. You wouldn't recognise true emotion if it hit you in the face.'

She made for the door, but Rex barred her way. 'Just where do you think you're going?'

'To get the hell out of here—and away from you.'

'Oh, no, you're not. Not until you've listened to me.'

'Sorry,' she almost snarled at him, 'but you've already said more than enough to last me the rest of my life. I'm going.'

'No, you're damn well not!' Rex caught hold of her, roughly pulling her back when she tried to break free, and held her arms in his strong grip. 'You won't leave. You can't. You want to go to bed with me too much. Don't you? Don't you?' And he kissed her with savage intensity, seeking to dominate her senses, to subdue her anger under physical need and desire. His mouth took hers in bruising passion as he tried to make her again a willing slave to his lovemaking.

Harry stood quite still, not responding, and at last he raised his head to look at her. Her face was very white and her eyes as cold as flint. 'Let me go,' she demanded tonelessly.

For a moment his hands tightened and she thought he was going to kiss her again, but then he gave a small shrug and stepped back. 'OK, if that's what you want.' His dark eyes challenged hers. 'If you *really* want to leave.'

Stepping past him into the sitting-room, Harry looked round for her handbag. 'Oh, I'm going all right. I only wish the film was over and I never had to see you again.'

'Yeah?' Rex leaned against the door jamb in insolent ease. 'Who are you trying to kid? You'll be back,' he said with certainty.

'No!' She swung round to face him, her eyes wide and vulnerable in her pale face. 'No...'

Rex laughed cruelly. 'Sure you will. Because you've had a taste of what it could be like. You may be mad now, but pretty soon you're going to realise just what you're missing, and then you're going to *beg* me to take you back.'

Harry shook her head wordlessly, then, unable to stand any more, she turned and ran out of the flat, fled down the stairs and into the street, to run to where the car was parked.

'Harry! Harry, wait!'

She heard Rex's shout behind her but ran on, turning to plunge into the street and dodge through the snarling congestion of traffic, the driver of a red double-decker bus hooting at her angrily as he braked to avoid her. The car was parked some distance away, but she didn't stop running until she reached it, only then realising that in her flight she had left her handbag and suitcase behind. Luckily she had kept the car-keys in the pocket of her skirt instead of putting them in her handbag, so she was able to get in and drive away, still half-afraid that Rex would come after her.

Not until she was several miles away from the Kensington area did her fear begin to recede. She wouldn't have put it past Rex, if he'd caught her, to have just slung her over his shoulder and carried her back to the flat and to that bed. What might have happened then she didn't care to think about, but she was so angry that she knew she would have fought him every step of the way, even if her body turned traitor and wanted him to go on. As soon as she reached a quiet stretch of road, Harry pulled up and tried to compose herself, but her brain was still seething with anger and humiliation. Oh God, she'd been such a fool! Harry's face burned as she remembered the way she'd let Rex handle her, and how ready she'd been to surrender herself to him. If she hadn't made that chance remark about the flat... She shuddered, realising how close she'd been. But she had been so sure that he was in love with her. Anger filled her veins, momentarily driving out the hurt pride and pain. How dared Rex make an announcement like that and still expect her to go to bed with him? It made her feel cheap, and belittled what she felt for Rex, too, making that seem immoral and nasty. But it *wasn't* like that. She could love him, if only he would let her.

Harry leant her forehead against her hands on the steering wheel, feeling slightly sick. All along she had been afraid that Rex had no real feelings for her, but these last few days she had really begun to be sure that he loved her. And now he had thrown it all back in her face!

She sat there for a long time, until she was startled by someone banging on the window and looked up to see a traffic warden looking in on her. 'You all right, love?' the woman called out.

Harry lowered her window and put a hasty hand up to wipe her eyes. 'Yes. Yes, I'm all right, thank you.'

'You don't look it,' the woman commented. 'Some rotten man, is it? You don't want to 'ave anything to do with 'em, ducks. That's my advice. They're all rotten, the lot of 'em,' she said, with the depth of feeling that could only come from personal experience. She gave a big sigh, then suddenly switched to being businesslike. 'I can't let yer stay 'ere any longer, love; you've 'ad your twenty minutes and more.'

'All right, thank you.' For some reason the unknown woman's tirade against the whole male gender made Harry feel a little better. She started up the car to pull away, but then realised that she couldn't go home because Rex had her handbag with her keys in it, and was bound to go there to find her. So the only place she could go to was her family home. Luckily, she still had one of her suitcases in the car, so she would have some clothes to wear, but she would just have to keep her fingers crossed that she had enough petrol in the tank to get there, because she certainly didn't have any money to buy some more.

She made it, but only just; the petrol indicator arm had been on empty for the last three miles as she turned at last into the driveway. Her parents were surprised, but pleased to see her, but she had to lie and pretend that she'd left her handbag behind in London so that she could borrow some money from them. That weekend she didn't help with the car, much to everyone's astonishment. Instead, she went off on her own for a long walk through the summer countryside. Her parents were sensitive people and knew that something was wrong with their only daughter, but were far too experienced to try to force her confidence; if she wanted to confide in them they knew she would do so in her own good time. But this was something Harriet knew she would have to get through on her own; having an affair with someone like Rex wasn't the kind of thing she could possibly ask her parents' advice about!

Usually she went back to London on Sunday night, but this weekend she spent Sunday night at her parents' house and went straight to the studios on Monday morning. She didn't have to appear in the first scene, so didn't arrive until nearly ten, nodding to the receptionist and going straight to her dressing-room. She had hardly been there two minutes before Rex strode in. He didn't knock or anything, just marched in and closed the door firmly behind him.

Harry gave him one glance then turned away. 'Would you mind knocking before you come into my room?' she said coldly.

'I want to talk to you, Harry,' Rex said grimly.

'Well, I have nothing to say to you,' she retorted before he could go on. 'Whatever was between us is over, finished. So would you please go away?'

'No, I damn well won't!' Putting his hand on her shoulder, he swung her round to face him. 'Where did you go over the weekend? Why didn't you call me? You could have got yourself killed, running through the traffic that way. I didn't know what had happened to you.'

'Your concern is, of course, extremely flattering,' Harry said with heavy sarcasm, completely ignoring the note of angry relief in his voice, 'but it's too damn late. We're through, Rex. So just get out of my room.'

'The hell I will!' Taking hold of her other arm, he held her in a tight grip. 'We're far from through. Do you really think I give up that easily? I want you, Harry, and I'm not going to let any misunderstanding come between us.'

Harriet laughed in his face. 'Misunderstanding, do you call it? Oh, no, I understood full well. And if you think that I'm going to—to live with you on your terms, then you're crazy.'

'All right. On what terms, then? If you won't accept mine, then name yours. Maybe I'll be more willing to accept them, whatever they are,' Rex said furiously, adding sardonically, 'I'm not an unreasonable man. Everyone has a price and...'

Lifting her hand, Harry hit him as hard as she could across the face. Unfortunately, Rex was too alert and saw it coming, so he was able to jerk his head back and avoid the full impetus, but he still felt it. 'Get out of here,' Harry bit out, shaking with fury and hardly able to control her anger. 'Just get out of my life!'

Rex's face beneath the film make-up had gone very white. His rage matching hers, he took a menacing step towards her and Harry hastily backed away, suddenly very aware of his towering strength.

'Miss Sutton.' One of the runners knocked and put her head round the door. 'They're ready for you in hairdressing.'

'Th-thank you,' Harriet managed in a choked voice. 'Wait a minute, will you?' she added quickly as the girl turned to go. 'I'd like you to do something for me.'

'Yes, of course.' The girl came into the room and looked at them curiously.

Rex gave Harry a fulminating glare that told her as plain as words that he was far from finished with her, and strode out of the room. Harriet would very much have liked to collapse on to the daybed, but she had to think up an errand for the runner to do, and then hurry to have her hair and face done. At least this gave her some time to recover, so that she was outwardly quite composed when she walked on to the set. It was as hot and busy as usual, the great lights burning down as everyone worked as fast as possible to keep up with the rigorous shooting schedule. She might have been mistaken, but Harry thought that the level of noise faded a little when she walked on, then picked up again. Instead of going to her chair, which had been placed beside Rex's as usual, she went over to talk to an actress that she knew from a previous television play, who had a small part as a policewoman.

The director was talking to his assistant, but soon came over and went through the scene she was to play with Emma and the actors playing police officers. Emma raised her eyebrows at her and mouthed, 'What happened?' but Harry shook her head and it wasn't until they were waiting to actually shoot the scene that Emma got her on her own. 'What happened between you and Rex?' she asked excitedly.

Harriet shrugged. 'Nothing much. Why?'

'Oh, come off it, Harry. Something must have happened between you. Rex came round to the house on Saturday, demanding to know where you were. Eric told him you weren't there, of course, but he just barged in and searched the place. Then said he was going to wait for you and refused to leave. Eric and I went out and he was still there when we got back at gone midnight. He left then, but he kept phoning up all day on Sunday to see if you were there.' She looked at Harry shrewdly. 'Did you two have a lovers' quarrel?'

Harry's face tightened. 'You could hardly call it a *lovers*' quarrel. We just had a blazing row, that's all.'

'What about?'

'Nothing you'd be interested in,' Harry said firmly. 'But it's over, that's definite.'

Emma chuckled richly. 'Not if Rex has anything to do with it, it's not. If he wasn't still mad about you he wouldn't have come round to the house and made all those phone calls.'

Harriet gave her a look and walked over to get herself a cup of coffee from the trolley. While she drank it she chatted to one of the production staff, carefully turning her back on Rex when he came over.

'OK, we'll shoot that scene,' the director called a few minutes later. 'You ready, Harry? Emma?'

They worked on till lunch time, which Harry took in her dressing-room. Now that Julie and the American actress had been killed off, she and Emma no longer had to share, so she was able to go in to her room and lock the door. When someone knocked about twenty minutes later, she suspiciously asked who it was, but it was only a runner who handed her a sealed envelope. Inside was a note from Rex. It began, 'Harry, honey. We have to talk this through.' She didn't read any more, just screwed the note up and threw it into the waste-paper basket. Then she grew afraid that one of the cleaners might read it, so she fished it out again and stuffed it into the bottom of her make-up box that she kept in the dressing-room, under all the bottles and tubes.

That afternoon she was to play a scene with Rex, in which he was to get very angry with her because she still refused to give him any information about his dead fiancée. The scene was to be played in the semi-darkened corridor leading up to the flat and he was supposed to get so mad with her that he was to use force to try and get her to talk.

The director called them on to the set and said, 'Do you two want to go and rehearse this on your own?'

'Sure,' Rex agreed.

'No,' Harry said at the same time, adding, 'I'd—I'd like you to go through it with us, if you don't mind.'

Looking at Rex's grim face and Harry's cold one, the director drew his own conclusions. 'OK, we'll talk it through. Now, Rex, you're waiting for Harry in the corridor. She steps out of the lift and you come up and get hold of her so that she can't get away. Then you start asking her questions, but she won't answer you, tells you you're becoming a bore. You know how to do that, Harry—be really cold and snooty. Very English. All right, we'll rehearse it that far.'

They did so, but both of them were too much aware of each other as people to bury their feelings completely while they acted. Rex's voice was rougher and his face grimmer than it need have been, and Harriet was too nervous.

'No, Harry, you're not afraid of him at first, just disdainful. And you've got to look at him, not avoid his eyes. But otherwise it's fine,' the director encouraged. 'Now, Rex, when she refuses to speak to you, you push her back against the wall and hold her, telling her that that's how your girl would have felt when *she* was killed. You're going to take your time about it, increasing the pressure slowly and keeping your voice low and menacing so that you don't rouse the neighbours, until you suddenly realise what you're doing and let her go. Then you carry her into the flat, put her on the bed. You talk and she gives you a letter that your fiancée wrote to you but was never posted. OK, go ahead.'

When actors rehearsed or played an angry scene, they were always careful not to hurt one another and Rex was careful now, but for all that Harry could feel the tension in his hands as he held her. She stared up into his eyes, trying to act but intensely aware of the desire in his face and the way he held her when he picked her up and carried her to the bed.

'Fine,' the director called when they'd done. 'OK, take a break while we go through the movements for lighting and sound. We'll use the stand-ins for this, while you two have a rest.'

He moved away and Harry went to go to her dressing-room, but Rex came up beside her and blocked the way. 'Let's go outside for some fresh air,' he ordered in an undeniable tone, and, taking her hand firmly in his, he led her out of the studio into the open. 'Did you get my note?' he demanded as soon as they were out of any-one's hearing.

'Yes. But I tore it up.' Pulling her hand free of his undermining hold, she looked away and said, 'I didn't even read it. There wasn't any point. I don't want to see you again, Rex. I'm not—I'm not interested any more.'

'Don't be so darn stupid!' he answered heatedly. 'We could work this out in two minutes, if you'd just give us a chance. Let's stop at the pub on the way home tonight so that we can...'

'No!' Harry broke in vehemently. 'It wouldn't be any good. We both have different values. We're just—just incompatible.'

'That's just a word,' Rex said disgustedly. 'If you think about it, no two people in the world are completely in-compatible. And we're certainly not, not where it matters. We want each other, Harry, we both know that. Why don't you admit it, and come and live with me?'

'No.' She shook her head. 'Your values are upside-down. Living together should come out of—of love and respect.'

'But I do respect you,' Rex said earnestly.

'No, you don't,' she retorted with a mirthless laugh. 'All you're interested in is sex. I was stupid enough to think otherwise. But people don't change. Not people like you.'

'What's that supposed to mean?' Rex demanded, a threatening note in his voice.

'Everything the papers say about you is true. You *are* nothing but a playboy. You'd just use me and then walk away without a backward glance. You don't care how you hurt anyone, because you haven't any feelings. Not real feelings. You just see something you want and you...' Harry's voice died in her throat. Rex had turned on his heel and walked away from her, his shoulders tense and his hands balled into tight fists at his sides.

Slowly, Harriet followed him back to the studio and waited quietly in a corner until she was called on to the set. There was a deadness in her eyes, but the make-up girl put some drops in them to make them sparkle. The clapper-board boy stood in front of the camera, it sounded and he quickly moved away. The director called 'Action!' and she opened the doors of the lift to step out into the corridor.

Rex grabbed her arm with a forcefulness that had no acting in it at all. There was a pinched look about his mouth and he fired the questions at her. Catching his anger, Harry answered him as if she really despised him, her tone as cold and cutting as a knife-blade. Rex, too, knew it was for real, and he pushed her back hard against the wall. His hands took hold of her, and she saw the scarcely controllable anger that flamed in his eyes. He was leaning against her, his body pressed on to the length of hers. He spoke his lines as they'd rehearsed them, but she knew that they were only a means of revealing his own fury. His fingers tightened, and a lick of fear ran through her. And with it a kind of fascinated excitement, because she'd made him so angry. If she could rouse him to feel this much anger, couldn't he also feel this much love? But there was sweat on his brow now, and his hands had tightened again and he was almost beginning to really hurt her.

'Damn you, you beautiful bitch,' Rex quoted viciously. 'I'll make you tell me what I want. Are your senses starting to go? Are you feeling the terror that she felt? Tell me, Harry, damn you! Tell me!'

'Cut!' The director's voice broke through the tension. 'You called her Harry, Rex. Otherwise it was great, perfect. The best piece of acting the two of you have done.'

Rex blinked and slowly straightened up, taking his weight off her. Harriet's eyes were closed and her face was completely colourless. She felt Rex remove his hands and slowly opened her eyes to see him staring at her, his face as white as hers.

'Harry.' He reached out towards her, but she gave a sob and pushed past him to run off the set and into her dressing-room.

'Harry, are you all right?' Emma quickly followed her in, closing the door behind her.

'Yes. I'm OK.' Harry turned to look at her reflection in the huge, light-bulb-lined mirror and saw red marks on her skin where Rex had held her. 'They—they'll show, won't they?' she asked rather unsteadily.

'You should be able to disguise them. I'll get the make-up girl, shall I?'

'No! No—you do it for me, will you? Please?'

'OK.' Emma sat down beside her and set to work. 'Rex really got carried away, didn't he? Do you want a drink? I've got a bottle of gin in my dressing-room.'

Harriet shook her head. 'No, thanks. I'm all right. Really. Rex squeezed a bit hard, that's all.'

Finishing her work, Emma stood back to look at her. 'That should do it.' Then she added abruptly, 'I was watching while they were shooting that scene, and I don't think either of you were acting. The anger you put into it was real, wasn't it?'

'Perhaps we're just both better actors than you think,' Harry returned lightly. But, seeing that the other girl was still frowning, added, 'Oh, OK, maybe we were angry with each other, but please don't make something more of it than it is.' Then she firmly led the way back on to the set.

Coming over to her, the director said, 'OK. You ready to try it again?'

Harry nodded and moved over to take her place behind the lift doors. The clapper-board sounded, the lift doors opened and she stepped out of them. Rex strode forward to catch hold of her, his face so bleak that she forgot her first line. They tried a second time, but Rex was so nervous of hurting her that it showed. They must have retaken the scene ten times, but neither of them could do it, the tension between them increasing with every take. In the end the director abandoned it for the day and told them to take it from where Rex carried her into the bedroom.

The action started, and he caught her as she slumped against the wall, then picked her up easily in his strong arms. It was heaven and hell to be held so close to him. Harry wanted desperately to put her arms round his neck and touch him, to see the light of desire in his eyes as she lifted her head to kiss him. But all she could do was to lie still in his arms and act her part. He put her down on the bed and she looked at him with animosity, then watched him walk away when she'd at last given him the information he wanted. Somehow it seemed symbolic, when he walked away, and Harry lay on the bed with her eyes closed after the director called 'Cut!'

He looked at her for a moment and then reached what must have been an unwelcome decision. 'OK, everybody, it's a wrap. Let's all go home and get an early night.'

With a sigh of relief, Harriet went to her room to change and cream off the heavy make-up. She had almost finished when there was a knock on her door and the director came in. He was a well known name in the screen world, and Harry had been a little nervous of him at first, but by now they were on friendly, first-name terms. 'How are you feeling?' he asked.

'Oh, fine, thanks. I'm—I'm sorry we weren't able to shoot that scene again.'

He gave her a long look under his thick eyebrows. 'What is this between you and Rex?'

Harry laughed and shrugged. 'Why, nothing! What should there be?'

'That's exactly what he said. And you're both lousy liars. But whatever it is, Harry, it's got to be settled, and quickly. I'm not going to let your personal differences interfere with the making of this film. Do you understand? The two of you have got to get together and sort yourselves out, one way or another. Whatever it is has got to be behind you when you come on to this set tomorrow. OK?'

Harry gulped at the thought of having to face Rex, but nodded. 'OK.'

'Good girl. And don't forget that this film is very important to your career. So far, I've been more than happy with your performance, so don't spoil it by letting personal emotions come into it.' He stood up and turned to go, but then hesitated. 'Harry, you're a nice kid. You know what Rex's reputation is like. I—well, I wouldn't want to see you get hurt.' Then he gave a brusque nod and went away.

Well! He could hardly have given her a more direct warning to keep well clear of Rex, but she had already made up her mind to that, anyway.

Emma was waiting in the car park and they drove home in silence, Emma tactfully refraining from pushing the questions she was longing to ask. The four of them ate together that evening, but then Bob went off to meet his current girlfriend and Emma and Eric went out for a walk by the canal bank in the warm evening sunset. They asked Harry to go with them, but she refused, preferring to be alone, and anyway loath to play gooseberry to what looked as if it might lead to an interesting romance between the two.

There was also the problem of obeying the director's instructions, but when Harry thought about it she realised that everything had already been sorted out; she had told Rex it was over and that was the end of their very brief affair, as far as she was concerned. This cowardly thought proved a great relief, and she just hoped that Rex would reach the same decision and not make any attempt to contact her. But then she remembered that she had left her handbag and a suitcase behind in his flat. Damn! Harriet bit her lip in vexation. Not having her cheque book and credit cards was a nuisance, not to speak of all the other things she habitually carried in her bag, but she was blowed if she was going to go round to Rex's flat to ask for them back. If he was any kind of a gentleman he would send them round. But right now Rex was a very angry man indeed, and not at all disposed to act like a gentleman towards her. Oh, well, if he didn't send her things back she would just have to send Eric or Bob—or, better still, both of them—round to the flat to get them for her.

Going upstairs, Harry had a leisurely shower and washed her hair, then came down to watch the television, but she couldn't settle. The evening was warm and she felt restless and lonely, wishing now that she'd gone with Emma and Eric. At least they could have sat outside one of the canalside pubs and had a drink. There would have been people and talk and laughter. She wouldn't have been stuck here with nothing to do but think about Rex and the fury in his eyes as he'd taken hold of her.

Suddenly making up her mind, Harry turned off the television and ran into the hall to pick up her jacket, impulsively deciding, in a defiant kind of mood, that she just couldn't stay in the house any longer. She pulled the front door shut behind her and only then remembered that she had no key to get back in with. Well, she would just have to stay out until the others came home.

Turning to go down the steps, she stopped as a taxi pulled up outside and Rex got out.

Harry could have turned and run away from him in either direction, but the sight of him standing there by the cab, looking up at her with such a bleak look on his face, made her legs go suddenly weak. So she just stood and waited until he'd paid off the cab and come over to her, carrying her case and a plastic shopping-bag that presumably contained her handbag.

For a moment they continued to stand and gaze at each other, until Rex said harshly, 'I brought your things back.'

His brusqueness drove away any softer feelings, so that she replied with equal coldness, 'Thank you.'

He hesitated for a moment, apparently at a loss. 'The director advised that we—we talk, sort things out.'

'Yes, he told me that, too,' Harry acknowledged, but she went no further to help him.

'Well, could we go inside and discuss it? Or would you rather we had it out here on the sidewalk?' Rex added sharply, when she didn't answer at once.

Harriet's face tightened. 'I don't have a key. Is my bag in there?' She indicated the plastic bag.

He handed it to her so that she was able to unlock the door and go back inside. Rex dumped her case in the hall and followed her into the sitting-room.

'Were you just going out?'

'Yes.'

Rex's eyes narrowed, and he looked as if he would have liked to ask her where she was going, but he merely said, 'I guess the director said more or less the same to you as he did to me. Only he laid into me a lot harder.'

'What else did he say?'

'That we had to work things out. Not let it interfere with our work. That kind of thing.'

'He said that to me, too. But he was mistaken; there is nothing to sort out,' Harry said coldly.

'What do you mean?'

'I told you this morning; it's over.'

'Look, if it's because I went too far when we were acting...'

'No!' She almost shouted the word at him, adding, as if it were torn out of her, 'For a while I was glad that you did. At least it showed that you were capable of some real feelings. But even that was for the wrong reasons. You were only mad at me because you couldn't have what you wanted. Like a child who's been promised a toy and then has it taken away from him.'

'That isn't so.' Rex took an urgent step towards her and reached out to take her arm, but stopped when she flinched away, his hands balling into knuckled fists. 'OK, I was mad at you. Really mad. A guy's entitled to get mad, the way you throw insults around. Look——' his voice became persuasive '—just because I don't want to commit myself on a permanent basis doesn't mean that I don't feel anything for you.'

Harriet gave a sniff of derision. 'The only thing you feel is lust!'

His mouth thinning into a grim line, Rex retorted sharply, 'Yeah, that's right. I do lust after you, God help me. I want to go to to bed with you more, I think, than any woman I've ever known. And it isn't because you've held me at arm's length for so long. Other girls have tried that trick on me, and it hasn't worked. If they play that hard to get then to hell with them; I'm not that hard-up. But you...' He gave an almost despairing shake of his head. 'I can't get you out of my mind. A dozen times since Saturday I've said, to hell with you. But then I remember what it was like when you were in my arms, and I start wanting you all over again.'

His words aroused her, because Harry, too, remembered the overwhelming ecstasy of his lovemaking, his sure expertise that had so inflamed her senses. But that expertise had come from his knowledge of many women.

Rex came up close to her, his eyes fixed on her face. Slowly, almost tentatively, he lifted his hand to touch her cheek. 'Let's go back to that time when we were in the flat together on the bed. Let's forget everything that's happened since then. You know you want to, Harry,' he tempted.

Harry jerked her head away. 'You're asking the impossible. There's no way I can forget.'

'Hell, do you have to be so damn stubborn?' Rex put his hands on her arms, somehow containing his strength and his anger, afraid of hurting her. 'I'm going crazy for you. Isn't that enough?'

'Oh, you poor thing,' Harry answered tauntingly. 'Why is that, I wonder? Because you haven't had a woman since you left the States? A whole month ago! My God, to be that frustrated you must be half-way to insanity by now!'

'Why, you little...' His jaw hardened in fury, Rex pushed her away. 'You really know how to take it out of a man, don't you?' For a moment he paused, striving to control himself. 'All right, maybe I do deserve to be punished for hurting you, but you sure as hell know how to hit back. But I wonder if it's just me you're punishing, or yourself as well. You may put on this cold-as-ice act, but deep down you're as hot-blooded as the next woman. We turn each other on, Harry, so why the hell can't we just go to bed and enjoy each other?'

Harry bit her lip, knowing that a lot of what he said was true, but she shook her head. 'I can't. I'm not going to let you—just use me like that. If you really cared enough to...' She stopped, knowing it was useless.

Rex's eyes narrowed. 'Is marriage what you want, what you were hoping for?'

'Oh, no, that's the last thing I expected,' Harry answered with a harsh, bitter laugh. 'The great Rex Kynaston—married! You'd probably lose half your fan club overnight. Oh, no, I had no illusions about that. What I did expect was that you would *care* about me, as well as just want me. That I would be a person to you, not just another—another female body. I hoped that I would *mean* something to you. That we could be friends as well as lovers. I didn't...' She put a hand up to her forehead. 'I didn't expect it to go on for ever. You see how few illusions I had,' she pointed out grimly. 'But I did hope that it would be a loving, caring relationship, that it wouldn't be just sex for sex's sake.' Agitatedly, she turned away, unable to go on.

'Why do you denigrate sex so much?' Rex asked curtly. 'It's the most important part of any relationship. You can build a basis on that as well as anything else.'

Scornfully she turned to face him again. 'Can you? I doubt it! To you, women are just sex objects; either the right age and shape or not. And that's all. They don't mean anything to you as people.'

'You're wrong,' Rex exclaimed heatedly. 'You're *not* just a body to be used. I *don't* look on women like that.' He looked at her angrily, then burst out, 'And I do care about you—very much.'

Harry laughed in his face. 'How can you possibly say that, when you've already said that it's going to end when you go back to America? You can't stop caring the way you stop water coming out of the tap when you turn it off.'

'But you said you didn't want to go to America with me. And you were willing enough until I wouldn't commit myself. What was it that upset you so much, Harry? Because you realised that I wouldn't marry you?'

He said it so sneeringly that Harry's face flushed. 'No. Even though I knew it couldn't last, I suppose that up until then I'd been carried along by my own—my own emotions. I was in love with you, and I thought—I believed—that you loved me.'

His face tightening, Rex said curtly, 'OK, so you wanted romance and I didn't give it to you. I'm sorry. I thought you were experienced and sophisticated enough to go into it with your eyes open. You certainly gave that impression.' He paused, then said on a note of urgent pleading, 'Look, nothing alters the fact that we have this basic chemistry going for us, Harry. We struck sparks off each other the moment we met. I want you more than I ever did and I know you feel the same, however much you try to deny it. If we don't go to bed together, we're going to regret it for the rest of our lives. And I do care about you. Would I have come round here like this if I *didn't* care?'

Harriet looked at him for a long moment, but shook her head. 'You might be telling yourself that. You might even believe it's true. But all you really want is to—to have me. I don't believe that you have any real feelings for me at all. And I don't really think that you feel any differently about me from all your other women. You're just obsessed with me at the moment, because I didn't fall for you straight away and because I refused to be— to be treated just as a sex object.'

'That isn't true.' Striding forward, Rex caught hold of her wrist. His face taut, his voice harsh and pleading, he said fiercely, 'I ache for you, Harry. Do you know what it's like to actually *ache* for someone? To wake up with this feeling deep in your stomach, so bad that it's like a pain that only grows. It *hurts*, Harry. It doesn't go away. It keeps me awake at night. And when I touch you it's as if someone had stuck a knife into my gut.' His hand tightened on her, but Harriet stood quite still, gazing into his face speechlessly. 'But no, you wouldn't know about that, would you? You say you want romance, but you can switch your emotions on and off like a tap. You want me, but that cold little brain of yours has decided that it has been insulted and nothing is going to make you change your mind.'

Letting go of her, he strode towards the door. 'OK, if that's the way you want it. If we'd got together it would have been really something.' He grinned mirthlessly. 'Who knows, we might really have made the earth move. It sure would have been a hell of a lot of fun finding out. But stay on your ice pedestal, Harry. Only be careful when you're ready to step down off it you don't find that you're frozen solid!'

CHAPTER EIGHT

THE next morning, both Rex and Harry kept as far away from each other as possible, and were icily polite when they had to speak. They went through the scene in the corridor again and it was a take first time. Both of them acted very professionally, simulating emotions that they were very careful not to actually feel.

The director nodded, satisfied that they had taken his advice, and aware that in this mood they would both work hard to get the film finished as quickly as they could, so that they could see the back of each other. Not one to miss an opportunity, the director decided to shoot another scene in which they were to appear together. To Harry's dismay, it was a strong emotional scene. 'I—I thought we weren't going to do that until tomorrow,' she objected.

'But we got through the last take so quickly that we have time to do it this morning. And as it's one of the last scenes to be actually shot in the studio, I'd like to get it out of the way. Any objections, Rex?'

'No, I guess I know the lines.'

'Do you, Harry?'

'Yes, of course. I—OK, let's go ahead.'

'Fine.' The director picked up his script. 'This is where Rex comes to the flat and tells you that he's fallen for you. You'll have to remember, Rex, that Harry is supposed to be a cold, upper class English girl, so she'll . . .'

'You don't have to tell me,' Rex interrupted grimly. 'I know all there is to know about cold English girls.'

The director stared at him, taken aback by the vehement bitterness in his tone, and for a moment there was a little shocked silence among those around them. Harriet looked fixedly down at her script, two bright spots of colour high on her cheeks.

Recovering, the director said, 'OK, we'll run it through, then.'

They rehearsed the lines and their positions, without actually touching each other, although some of the lines they had to say were so close to the truth that Harry could hardly bear to look at Rex as she spoke them. Overnight, she had managed to talk herself into an uncompromising frame of mind, one in which she found the necessary resolve to resist any further approaches that Rex might make. But as Rex behaved towards her with remote indifference she wasn't called on to use it. Not, at least, until they had to play that scene. And then it was her own weakness that she had to fight, not Rex.

Just seeing him had made her heart start to beat faster, and roused an ache of awareness in the pit of her stomach. Last night Rex had said that he ached for her, but it worked both ways, unfortunately. She took a sneaking look at him when they were standing close together waiting for the lights to be adjusted, and saw the rock-hard set of his jaw beneath his tight mouth. Instinctively she guessed that he, too, was having to fight hard to maintain his attitude of remoteness. She could smell the early-morning, clean aroma of his aftershave and see the thin material of his shirt stretched tight across his broad chest. His jeans, too, weren't exactly loose.

The director called him over for a minute and he turned and stood with his back to her. He had a broad back and powerful shoulders, making Harry remember how strong and yet how gentle he could be.

Rex finished speaking to the director and moved to return to his place. His cold eyes glanced at her as he did so, and he stopped short, his eyes gazing arrestedly at her face. Harriet had no idea how sensuous she looked right at that moment, when she was off guard. Her eyes betrayed her the most, the deep longing in their hazel depths plain to see, but edged with the dark shadows of unhappiness and loss. Her mouth, too, gave her away. Her lips were slightly open, like those of a woman waiting to be kissed, the lower one full and trembling. It struck Rex that her face was like that of a woman who looks up at her lover, waiting for him to take her, for the first but also for the last time. He was filled with a violent urge to pick her up in his arms and carry her to the nearest place where they could be alone. To break through every barrier of resistance and coldness and to make her cry out with pleasure as he thrust his body into hers. To drive out the unhappiness from her face and replace it with desire and passion. To have her call his name again and again in an unquenchable frenzy of ecstatic pleasure. And to go on and on, to never stop loving her. And then to hold her, to hold her close and feel her heart beating against his.

'Rex?' The director spoke his name for the second time, and Rex slowly moved forward to take his place, beads of sweat on his forehead and beneath his moustache.

Deliberately sticking his hands in his pockets, Rex stood looking up at the high ceiling where all the lights were suspended on iron scaffolding, whistling tunelessly while they waited. Harry watched the crew at work, looked down at her marks on the floor, memorising them, looking anywhere but at Rex, but was so over-whelmingly aware of him that she saw everything else through a misty kind of haze.

'Are those lights ready yet?' the director called im-patiently. 'We're losing the time we made up.'

'Two minutes,' the technician called down. 'Just give me another two minutes.'

The director nodded grumblingly, his eyes on his two leading actors, who stood so tensely silent in the middle of the noisy set, waiting to play a scene that neither of them wanted to do. The two minutes seemed to go on endlessly, but at last the huge lights came on and the director gave a sigh of relief. 'All right, let's go. Now, remember, Rex, you've fallen for the girl but you're still not absolutely sure that she didn't have something to do with your fiancée's death. And Harry, you think he's making up to you just to get more information out of you.'

The clapper-board brought instant hush, in which a doorbell rang. Harry went to answer it and found Rex at the door, leaning on the jamb. 'What do you want?'

He shouldered his way in and they went on with the scene, Rex coming up behind her as she turned away and putting his hands on her shoulders. His touch made her gasp for real and, as she turned to tell him to go, it was as if it was last night all over again. Only now Rex had to touch her, to take her in his arms and kiss her, as he tried to convince her that he was telling the truth. As he held her, she could feel the tremors that ran through his body, saw the genuine desire in his eyes as he bent her back to kiss her, and tasted the flaming passion of his lips.

Playing her part, she fought him off and stood, her trembling in no way contained, as she accused him of deception and falsehood. The words came easily enough, but reality merged into pretence and she felt as if she was rejecting him all over again. Only this time it was doubly hard. Her body cried out for him and she wanted to run to him and hold him, to say, yes, yes, yes.

But instead she had to yell, 'Get out of here or I'll call the police! I mean it. Get out or I'll call them. You've made a nuisance of yourself once too often.' And to lift the telephone receiver threateningly.

Rex came up close to tower over her. He was shaking, but whether it was true or false, with anger or passion, she didn't know. 'You cold bitch!' he bit out forcefully. 'I wish to hell I *hadn't* fallen for you. Do you think it makes me happy, wanting you? Well, it doesn't! Not one bit! As soon as this is over I'm going back home to the States, and I'm going to forget I ever set eyes on you.'

He turned and strode off the set. The director called 'Cut!' but Harry still stood there, knowing that every word he'd said he'd meant. Feeling as if her heart had turned to stone.

That was the end of filming for the day for Harriet. She went home alone, making no attempt to see Rex, who had gone to the restaurant with a couple of male actors and some of the production staff. There was still

several days of filming to be done at the studios, but all
her scenes were with Emma or other people; she had
none with Rex. He was out on location with the second
unit, shooting scenes in which he was getting close to
the real murderer, so she didn't even see him. She heard
about him, though: how he had organised a party for
the location unit that had got out of hand. It hadn't
made any headlines, but it had cost a whole day's filming
while the crew recovered from their hangovers.

When the director heard about it, his face became grim
and he immediately left the studio to go and sort
everyone out, leaving the rest of the studio shooting in
the care of one of his assistants. There wasn't a lot left
to do; just a few odd scenes and a few filler shots, close-
ups and that kind of thing. It only took a few more days
and then Harry was free until her next location shots
were scheduled, in about three weeks' time. For Emma,
however, it was the end of her part in the film, as it was
for quite a few members of the crew. To celebrate, they
had their own party on the set the night before it was
to be broken up. It wasn't a bad party as parties go, but
Harry found that she just couldn't get into the swing of
things, partly, she supposed, because for her this wasn't
actually the end of the film, but mostly because she just
wasn't in the mood. She obligingly flirted a little with
one of the production staff who fancied her, but refused
his invitation to take her out for a meal.

'Have you got anything lined up?' she asked Emma
as they drove back to London later that evening.

'An audition for a voice-over in a television com-
mercial, that's all. I shall have to start chasing my agent
again.'

'Will you go back to Birmingham?'

'Well . . .' Emma looked at her sideways. 'As a matter of fact I've been thinking about that, and I wondered if you'd mind if I kept my room at the house on for a while. It might be better to be on hand if any work crops up.'

'Of course,' Harry agreed, adding with a smile, 'It couldn't be anything to do with Eric, could it?'

Emma laughed happily. 'Could be.' After a moment she said, 'Have you—er—heard from Rex?'

'No.' Harry shook her head, trying not to let any emotion show. 'I didn't expect to.'

'It's all over, then?'

'Yes, what there was of it. Which wasn't very much. It was one of those affairs that had to be all or nothing. And as we couldn't agree, it turned out to be nothing.'

'Isn't there any chance that you might get back together? You seemed—right for each other, somehow.'

Harry gave a bitter-sweet laugh. 'You mean, we both have flaming tempers?'

'No, that you're both too proud for your own good,' Emma told her roundly. 'You were obviously crazy about each other, and yet, when whatever it was went wrong, you were both so full of stubborn pride that neither of you would give way. What does it matter who's in the wrong?' she went on impatiently. 'You want him, don't you? And don't try to deny it, Harry; you've been mooning around like a lost sheep ever since he went on location.'

'All right!' Harry exclaimed. 'OK, I'm—I'm not trying to deny it. But it just didn't work, that's all.'

Emma snorted. 'Huh! Don't try to tell me that you gave Rex a fair chance, because I shan't believe you. You didn't want to fall for him in the first place, but when you did, you seized on the first thing that went wrong as an excuse to break it off, telling yourself that you'd been right all along and he wasn't the man for you. I don't call that giving it a chance.'

Astonished by the vehemence in her friend's voice, Harry just sat there speechlessly, wondering how much of it, if any, was true.

But it seemed that Emma wasn't content to leave it there. 'And what I want to know is, what are you going to do about it? It isn't too late, you can still make it up.'

'It is too late. He—he doesn't care about me.'

'Of course he does. He's mad about you.'

'He's mad about going to bed with me, that's all. He doesn't care about me as a person.'

'Well, as I said, you haven't given him a chance. If you started being a bit nicer to him, he might learn to care. I want you to promise me that when you meet him on location you'll try and make it up with him,' Emma insisted.

'No, definitely not. Just mind your own business, please, Emma.'

'No. Because I'm not going to let you throw away one of the best chances you'll ever get. If you won't promise, then I'll phone him up and tell him that you're still crazy about him.'

'He wouldn't believe you,' Harry returned with certainty.

'He would if I told him how you cry yourself to sleep every night.'

The car swerved into the kerb and Harry pulled up with a jerk. She turned to her friend, her face white and vulnerable. 'Oh, Emma!'

Leaning forward, Emma put a hand over hers. 'Harry, surely it's better to be unhappy with him than to go on like this. Promise me you'll try and make it up.'

Harry gazed down at her hands gripping the steering wheel, then slowly nodded. 'You're right. I was crazy to hope that he might...' She broke off, biting her lip. 'You promise you won't say anything to him, though.'

Emma smiled. 'OK. Good luck, Harry.'

'One way or the other,' Harriet answered grimly, 'I think I'm going to need it.'

So it was with very mixed feelings that Harriet drove down into Hampshire to join the film crew for the final location scenes in which she was to appear. The actual filming was to take place in quite a large house, set in its own grounds and in the woodland surrounding it, but the unit and actors had all been booked into a hotel a few miles away. It was a new location and all the members of the unit were due to check in on the Sunday evening, ready to start shooting early on Monday morning. It was a tense time for everyone, so near to the end of the film. There was still intense concentration needed, and yet there was also a sort of end-of-term feeling when professional attitudes relaxed a little and people played jokes on each other and were impatient of the long waits in between takes, which were always much longer on location than in the studio.

Some of the crew had already arrived at the hotel, and greeted her like a long-lost friend. There was plenty of news to catch up on, for a film unit was always a hotbed of gossip. During filming, as Harry now very well knew, relationships became very, very intense, and she and Rex hadn't been the only ones who had had something going for them.

She had dinner at the hotel and was afterwards having a drink in the bar with several members of the unit when Rex arrived. He strolled in in that gracefully casual way he had, and started to greet everyone: a slap on the back, a wave or a smile, a friendly word. But when he came to Harriet he gave her just a brief nod, and passed quickly on to the next person, afterwards going to sit with a few of the British male actors on stools at the bar.

Knowing that most of them had to be up by six, the group broke up fairly early and made their way up to their rooms. Harry found herself in the same lift as Rex, squashed in with about eight other people, but she and Rex were the only ones who got out on the third floor. Harry said a husky goodnight, without even looking at him, and walked quickly ahead down the corridor to her room, but fumbled in her bag for her key, her hand suddenly shaking. She heard the noise of another lock being turned and looked up to see that Rex was opening the door of the room next to her own! Their eyes met and he gave another brief nod before going inside. Somehow Harry managed to find her own key, but went more slowly into her room, turning to stare at the wall which divided them. It was the wall that the bed was against. It would be! And probably, being like most modern hotel rooms the world over, it meant that Rex's bed was against the same wall. They would be sleeping within a few feet of one another. If the wall hadn't been there they could have reached out and touched.

It didn't even occur to her to ask to change her room. Harry just lay in bed, thinking about Rex and wishing the night—and the wall—away.

The next day she had to play some scenes in the house, not with Rex, but with two new actors who were supposed to be her parents. They were both very experienced and the scenes were done quickly enough to please the director, but Harry was acutely aware of Rex sitting on the edge of the set, watching. It wasn't something that he had done very much at the studios, preferring to go to his dressing-room or outside the studio to wait. But here she felt his eyes fixed on her the whole time, even though he was sitting right at the back of the room, out of the way.

Then it was the turn of Rex to film some shots of him trying to break into the house and creeping through it, looking for her, only to be almost caught by her father and having to hurriedly leave.

The shooting went on late into the night as they tried to do as much of the night-time filming as they could. Everyone was short of sleep and showing it when the crew assembled the next day. Little niggly things started to go wrong, and tempers grew short. Even Rex got annoyed and told someone off when a prop he was supposed to pick up wasn't in its place. It was the first time since the film had started that Harry had ever heard him lose his temper, even as mildly as this, and she supposed that he, too, was suffering from the build-up of tension. But then he lifted his head and looked directly across to where she stood against the wall, his eyes scorching through her veins and setting her blood on fire. It was such an emotive look that for a moment Harry was too stunned to move, but then she quietly turned and left the set, realising that Rex must be as aware of her as she had been of him.

The day was fine and she sat on the grass outside, the scent of a bed of old roses sweet in her nostrils. She hadn't forgotten her promise to Emma, but how she was supposed to try to make it up with Rex when he wouldn't even speak to her she didn't know. Just go and knock on his door tonight and say, 'Here I am. Take me?' The thought brought a slightly embarrassed smile to her lips, and she wondered if that had ever happened to Rex before. Probably. It was the kind of thing that happened to sex symbols. Her eyes grew thoughtful. Did he object to being called that? Wasn't it as bad for a man to be treated as a sex symbol as it was for a woman to be just a sex object? Rex had said that he was keen for this film to be a success, so maybe he wanted to be known as an actor, instead. Maybe he was afraid of eventually becoming too old to go on with his macho male image. Lying back on the grass, Harry wondered when you got too old to be a sex symbol any more. Some of them seemed to go on for ever and ever. Harry's eyes closed, her mind wandering, and she fell asleep, not waking until someone's shadow blotted out the sun.

Slowly, she opened her eyes and blinked, moving languorously. A man stood over her, looming like a giant bird of prey, but she couldn't see his face properly because the sun was in the way. Then he moved and she saw that it was Rex. Her breath caught in her throat and she choked a little, sitting up hastily.

'Are you all right?'

'Yes. I—I was dreaming.'

'I came to tell you that the catering van has arrived.'

'Oh, thanks.'

He nodded and turned to walk back to the house before she could gather her wits and speak or go after him. But it was already too late; one of the wardrobe girls had gone to talk to him.

The crew again worked late that day, some of them filming, but others setting up parallel lines of rails in the woods on which they would run the dolly carrying the cameras for the next day's filming. Harry hung around later than she need have done, in the hope of having an opportunity to speak to Rex, but it seemed almost as if he regretted speaking to her earlier, because he kept well away for the rest of the day.

A lot of preparation had gone into the next day's shooting; it was to be one of the action highlights of the film, but Murphy's Law came violently into effect and it poured with rain the whole day. The producer went to check that his weather insurance was paid up, and everyone else just sat around in the vain hope that it would clear. Harry rather desperately looked for an opportunity to go and talk to Rex, but he had joined a group of men playing poker, and there was no way she could just go up to him in front of the whole crew and ask to speak to him privately.

It rained again all the next morning, the skies not clearing until almost lunch time. Harry stayed in her room at the hotel, not going to the location site until she was called. In her role that day she had to be out riding in some woodland when Rex appeared on the scene. She had to recognise him and deliberately ride her horse at him, but he was supposed to grab the reins and pull her off. And then they had to make love on the ground.

She wouldn't actually be riding the horse herself, of course; they had a stand-in to do that. And it wouldn't be Rex, but a stuntman who would reach up through the rearing hooves of the horse to grab the reins. But it would be them on the ground.

It was important for the safety of the stuntman that everything was timed and went exactly right. They went through it once without the horse actually rearing and then decided to shoot it, the two stand-ins looking remarkably like the actors, the woman with a wig exactly the colour and style of Harriet's hair, and wearing an identical riding jacket and breeches.

Harriet stood back, watching, her fingers crossed that the stuntman wouldn't get hurt. The girl appeared at the edge of the wood on a big chestnut horse and drove her knees into its sides, sending it galloping towards the stuntman. She came up to him and he stepped forward, the horse rearing up, its metal hooves flailing the air dangerously. But then the horse slipped on the muddy ground, it lost its balance and went crashing heavily down on to the ground, the girl beneath it!

There was a moment of stunned silence and then everybody seemed to move at once. The stuntman ran forward to catch the horse and pull it to its feet while Rex picked the girl up from under it and carried her out of the way. She lay in his arms, unconscious, her right arm hanging loosely at an unnatural angle.

'Oh God, her arm's broken!' someone exclaimed.

'Run to the house and call for an ambulance,' the director shouted at a hovering technician.

Rex laid her on a blanket, and it was he who ordered the carpenter to make some splints, and then carefully put her arm into a sling while they waited for the ambulance. The girl came round and began to cry with pain, her sobs tearing at all their hearts. Rex held her, gently stroking her and murmuring words of comfort.

The ambulance arrived at last and took her away, leaving a void of silence behind her, no one wanting to be the first to state the obvious. But it was the director, who had seen accidents happen before on a set, who did so. Turning to the stuntman he said, 'Is there any hope of getting a girl to replace her today?'

The man shook his head. 'I might be able to find someone in a couple of days.'

'The weather forecast is for rain then. Can't you get anyone? Are you sure?'

Silently the man shook his head.

'Damn! And we were on schedule, too.'

Harriet stepped forward and said into the dispirited silence, 'I could do it.'

'What?' The director swung round to look at her. 'You, Harry? You can ride?'

'Why, yes, I...'

'No!' Rex's voice cut sharply through. 'She isn't going to do it. It's too dangerous.'

'But if she says she can do it, Rex, I don't...'

'No,' Rex said again, striding forward belligerently. 'You've seen what happened to that other girl; how can you even consider letting Harry do it? Do you want her ending up with a broken arm—or worse, too?'

'We could make sure the ground isn't slippery by putting sand down,' the stuntman put in. 'The horse wouldn't slip again.'

'I've told you no. She isn't doing it, and *that's* an end to it,' Rex said forcefully. He swung round to face her. 'You're not doing it, do you understand?'

Harry was gazing up at him in amazement, her eyes brilliant. 'You *do* care,' she said on a low note of wonder.

Rex looked back at her and pushed a lock of hair off his forehead. 'Of course I damn well care!'

'Oh, Rex!' A lump of emotion came into her throat, and she reached out a hand towards him, but the director had seen a chance to get his scene shot and he wasn't going to just let it go.

'Why don't we just let her get on the horse?' he coaxed. 'Then we could shoot the bit where she comes out of the wood and sees you.' Getting hold of Rex's arm, he pulled him away and left his assistant talking to him persuasively. Coming back to Harry, he said urgently, 'Can you really ride?' Harry nodded. He said, 'Well enough to do that scene? Truly, now.'

'Yes,' she assured him. 'I've been able to ride ever since I can remember.'

'Could you do the fall as well? Where he pulls you off?'

She smiled. 'One more fall won't make much difference. And, anyway, the stuntman will catch me.'

'Do you want to rehearse?' She shook her head and he said, 'OK, do it then. Rex will probably skin me alive, though, when he knows about it.'

So Harry went up to the horse and talked to it for a while, getting to know the animal before she got on his back, afterwards taking him for a canter round a nearby paddock before going to take up her position in the woods.

She had to wait a little while before the runner standing beside her with a walkie-talkie got the go-ahead from the director. He nodded to her and Harry trotted the horse to the edge of the woods. The stuntman came into sight, looking remarkably like Rex, and she reined in the horse, then dug her heels into its flanks and went flat out at the man. The horse broke into a gallop and she got ready to make it rear as soon as they reached him. Harriet was concentrating on what she had to do, confident that both the horse and the stuntman were well trained for this kind of thing, and it wasn't until she was up quite close and it was too late to stop that she saw that it really *was* Rex.

Petrified that she might hurt him, Harry yanked harder on the reins than she would otherwise have done, and the poor horse reared up high, whinnying in fright, and trying to pivot on its hind legs to turn and gallop away. But Rex strode forward with complete confidence, grabbing the reins in one hand and Harry's arm in the other, pulling her off the horse so that she fell, as she was meant to, on to a thick foam pad covered with leaves.

Her surprise and horror at finding that it was Rex almost made Harry forget to act, but she remembered in time and started to struggle with him as he came to hold her down. They fought together, rolling on the ground, the wet leaves sticking to their clothes and hair. Harry gasped as he rolled on her and tried to hit him, but Rex caught her wrists, holding them above her head. His dark, hungry eyes gazed down into hers for a moment, and it was then that Rex stopped acting and began to kiss her for real, taking her mouth with the fierce need of a man who has been too long denied.

Harry forgot the rolling cameras and the watching crew, oblivious to everything but the overpowering need to respond to his kisses, to return them with all the desire and love that filled her heart. They rolled on the ground now not in anger but in passion, each fighting greedily to touch the other, to hold, to taste. Harry put her arms around his neck, her fingers digging into his back, while Rex kissed her with desperate longing, his lips finding her neck, her throat, her eyes. A gasping moan broke from him as he put a hand in her hair so that he could take her mouth again, kissing her so fiercely that she felt as if she was falling into an endless vortex of pleasure. Her body arched under his and he rolled over so that she lay on top, his hands still in her hair as he went on kissing her. Harriet moved voluptuously against him, the hardness of his body driving her mad with frustration. Putting a hand low on her hip, Rex pressed her against him and then rolled over again, his body straddling hers, their legs entwined. He went on kissing her hungrily, his hands moving over her, both of them completely unaware of everything else, not even hearing the director when he called out 'Cut!'

It was only when the crew began to laugh, clap and whistle approvingly, that Harry realised where she was and opened her eyes. 'Rex!' she murmured against his mouth, and tried to move her head away. He immediately pulled her back and it wasn't until she kept insistently pushing at him that Rex at last lifted his head and gave a long sigh. Rolling off her, he heaved himself to his feet, his back to the cameras, and pulled her up beside him. Harry was blushing furiously, but there was a great light of happiness in her face as she looked at him.

He saw it and his hand tightened. 'Are we OK now?' he asked urgently.

Harriet smiled and nodded, almost shyly. 'Yes, I—I think we are.'

Rex's face lit with a huge grin. 'About time.' And he pulled her to him and kissed her again in front of them all, afterwards putting his arms round her and hugging her tightly, while Harry buried her flaming face in his shoulder amid the cheers and applause of the crew.

'We-e-ell!' the director exclaimed. 'We certainly got more than we bargained for there.' They turned to find him smiling broadly. 'I take it you weren't hurt at all, either of you?'

They shook their heads and Harriet turned to Rex. 'But I don't understand why it was you and not the stuntman. It frightened me to death when I realised. What happened?'

'Nothing happened. I just decided that if you were going to do the scene yourself, then so was I.' He bent his head to murmur in her ear. 'But maybe I hoped that this would happen.'

Harriet put her arms round his waist and smiled mistily up at him. 'Was it worth the risk?'

'I'll say.' He kissed her ear deliciously. 'Let's go and talk.'

'Talk?' She raised a pert eyebrow.

'Well, we might get a couple of words in.'

Putting his arm round her waist, Rex began to walk with her towards the privacy of the woods, not stopping until they were well out of sight and sound of the film unit. They came to a clearing where sunlight sparkled on raindrops still clinging to the leaves and where the air was heavy with the rich, humid smell of damp undergrowth. There Rex stopped and gently put his arms round her, his dark eyes holding hers. 'I've missed you,' he said sincerely. 'Oh God, how I've missed you.'

'And I you,' Harry admitted. 'It's been—unbearable.' Lifting her hand, she touched his face lovingly, and Rex turned his head to bury his mouth in her palm, then pulled her to him and kissed her again, a long kiss of tenderness, without passion, but so full of emotion that it somehow went deeper than desire.

When he at last raised his head, Rex held her close and said raggedly, 'I love you, Harry. I know that now. But I was such a fool that I didn't realise it until you ran out on me. Even then I almost couldn't believe it, but I missed you more with every day that passed.' He gave a short laugh. 'If you only knew the number of times I went to pick up the phone and tell you.'

'But why didn't you? We could have been together.'

'Because I was afraid that you wouldn't believe me, that I was just saying it to get you to come back to the flat.'

'Oh, but I would never have done that,' Harry exclaimed.

'Why not? You had reason enough,' Rex said wryly.

'Rex, if you'd been the kind of man to stoop to something as underhand as that, then you'd have told me you weren't taking me back to the States with you *after* we'd been to bed, not before.'

'Thanks.' Rex's eyes crinkled into his special smile. 'I'm crazy about you, you know that?'

'I think you did mention it before.'

'But this time it's for keeps. I want you to marry me, Harry. I want us to be together always.' His eyes shadowed. 'But there's your career, your family.'

'Well, as far as my career is concerned it definitely takes second place now. Somehow ambition seems to fly out of the window when you fall in love. And, as for my family, well, I think it's high time they met you—and I'm sure we'll be able to come back often to see them, won't we?' she asked a trifle anxiously.

'Sure, maybe we'd even manage two homes and spend six months here and six in the States.'

'Why, that would be wonderful! Oh, Rex.' She put her arms round his neck to kiss him, and it was some time before they spoke again. Then Harry asked, 'Why *did* you take the stuntman's place this afternoon?'

'It was because of what happened to that girl,' Rex answered slowly. 'When I saw her lying there, she looked so like you. It made me realise how I'd feel if anything happened to you. If I lost you.' He paused for a moment, his jaw taut. 'I knew you wouldn't just ride up on the horse, that you'd be crazy enough to do the whole thing. And I decided that if anyone was going to get you off that horse before it had a chance of falling over again, it was going to be me.'

'You could have been hurt yourself.'

He shook his head, dismissing the idea. 'I've done plenty of stuntwork in the past. I just wanted to be sure you were safe.' Holding her close, his cheek against her hair, Rex said, 'You know something, these last few days have been some of the worst in my life.'

'Good heavens! Why?'

'I knew that I was in love with you, but I was afraid that I'd killed everything you'd felt for me. I'd made up my mind that I'd know the moment you came down here on location. I'd banked so much on that. And when you did arrive you seemed so cold and withdrawn. I wanted to tell you how I felt but I was afraid of getting my head blown off if I said anything.'

'Oh, dear!' Harry gave a gurgle of laughter. 'If you only knew how close I got to going to your room last night, knowing that you were sleeping just the other side of the wall.'

'Not sleeping,' Rex corrected. 'Lying there thinking about you and kicking myself for having been such an idiot. I've been doing quite a lot of that lately.'

'But you won't have to any more, will you?' Harry reminded him softly.

With a delighted laugh, Rex picked her up and swung her round in exuberant happiness. 'Oh, my sweet Harriet! I love you so much.'

'And I you, you big fool.'

His arms tightened around her. 'You sure you don't want to wait until we can get a special licence and get married?'

Such deep happiness filled her heart that Harry came close to tears, but she blinked and looked down at him threateningly. 'Listen, buster, if you think I'm going to wait until then, you're crazy. Just because you've suddenly become respectable doesn't mean that I have, too.' She smiled mistily at the man she'd tamed, and paused to let the words sink in. 'As far as you're concerned, Rex, my darling, my intentions have always been—distinctly dishonourable!' And she burst into a peal of happy laughter at his look of stunned surprise.

ATTRACTIVE, SPACE SAVING BOOK RACK

Display your most prized novels on this handsome and sturdy book rack. The hand-rubbed walnut finish will blend into your library decor with quiet elegance, providing a practical organizer for your favorite hard-or soft-covered books.

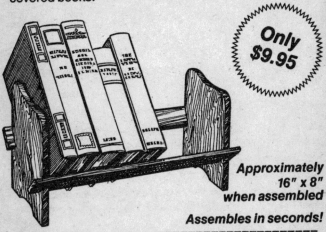

Only $9.95

Approximately 16" x 8" when assembled

Assembles in seconds!

To order, rush your name, address and zip code, along with a check or money order for $10.70* ($9.95 plus 75¢ postage and handling) payable to *Harlequin Reader Service*:

Harlequin Reader Service
Book Rack Offer
901 Fuhrmann Blvd.
P.O. Box 1396
Buffalo, NY 14269-1396

Offer not available in Canada.

*New York and Iowa residents add appropriate sales tax.

BKR-1A

Temptation™

TEMPTATION WILL BE
EVEN HARDER TO RESIST...

In September, Temptation is presenting a sophisticated new face to the world. A fresh look that truly brings Harlequin's most intimate romances into focus.

What's more, all-time favorite authors Barbara Delinsky, Rita Clay Estrada, Jayne Ann Krentz and Vicki Lewis Thompson will join forces to help us celebrate. The result? A very special quartet of Temptations...

- **Four striking covers**
- **Four stellar authors**
- **Four sensual love stories**
- **Four variations on one spellbinding theme**

All in one great month! Give in to Temptation in September.

Lynda Ward's

LEAP THE MOON

...the continuing saga of The Welles Family

You've already met Elaine Welles, the oldest daughter of powerful tycoon Burton Welles, in Superromance #317, *Race the Sun*. You cheered her on as she threw off the shackles of her heritage and won the love of her life, Ruy de Areias.

Now it's her sister's turn. Jennie Welles is the drop-dead-gorgeous, most rebellious Welles sister, and she's determined to live life her way—and flaunt it in her father's face.

When she meets Griffin Stark, however, she learns there's more to life than glamour and independence. She learns about kindness, compassion and sharing. One nagging question remains: is she good enough for a man like Griffin? Her father certainly doesn't think so....

Leap the Moon ... a Harlequin Superromance coming to you in August. Don't miss it!

LYNDA-1B